The Beginning

Look for other  titles by K.A. Applegate:

The Beginning

K.A. Applegate

AN
APPLE
PAPERBACK

SCHOLASTIC INC.
New York Toronto London Auckland Sydney
Mexico City New Delhi Hong Kong

Cover illustration by David B. Mattingly
Art Direction/Design by Karen Hudson/Ursula Albano

ISBN 0-439-11528-0

12 11 10 9 8 7 6   1 2 3 4 5 6/0

Printed in the U.S.A.
First Scholastic printing, May 2001

For Michael and Jake

The Beginning

CHAPTER 1

My name is Rachel.

I knew what was coming. I knew.

I'd seen it in Jake's eyes.

And you know what? I was scared.

I never thought I would be. Cassie thinks I'm fearless. Marco thinks I'm reckless. Tobias . . . well, Tobias loves me.

I guess they all do, in different ways. Jake, too. But Jake had to do the right thing.

I felt sorry for him, you know? He's carried the weight so long. He's made hard decisions. None as hard as this maybe. I didn't blame him, not even for a minute.

But I was scared.

1

I guess no one wants to die. I guess everyone is scared when the time comes.

We were so close. We were right there, right at the finish line, I'd already survived so many times when I shouldn't have. It seemed unfair. To come this far, get this close . . .

Jake gave me the job because he knew that only I could do it. Would do it. Ax might have, sure, but he was needed for his skills. Me, I'm not the computer genius. I'm the one you send when you need someone to be crazy, to do the hard thing.

I don't know whether I'm proud of that or not.

I was Jake's insurance policy. He thought maybe he wouldn't have to use me. He hoped, anyway. But down deep he knew, and I knew, and we both hid the truth from the others because Cassie couldn't let Jake make that decision, and Tobias couldn't let me, and those two, by loving us, would have screwed everything up.

It was a war, after all. A war we had to win.

We hadn't asked the Yeerks to come to Earth. They made that call on their own. They're a parasitic species, not very big or impressive to look at, just these snail-like things that can enter your head through your ear. They have a capacity to anesthetize the inner ear enough to allow them to burrow through the soft tissue. It still hurts but not as much as it should.

They dig their way straight to your brain and

2

then flatten themselves out, spread themselves down into the crevices, tie directly into your synapses. They take control. Absolute control.

They read your thoughts, they sense your emotions. What your eyes see, they see. What your tongue tastes, they taste. If your hand moves, it's because they moved it. If you speak, it is the Yeerk who has spoken through you, made you into a ventriloquist's dummy.

Over the course of years they spread like a virus. Invisible. Undetectable.

They are your teacher, your pastor, your best friend. They are the police officer, the TV newsman, the soldier. Anyone.

Jake's parents had recently been taken; they were human-Controllers — people controlled by Yeerks.

Jake's brother Tom, my cousin, had been a Controller for a long time. He was a powerful Yeerk. Jake still cared for him, still hoped somehow he could be saved.

Jake had sent me away with Tom.

I understood. I approved. If Jake hadn't sent me I'd have gone anyway.

Still, though, I was scared.

I had power myself. We all did. The strange, unsettling power to absorb DNA from any living creature, to then alter our physical bodies to become that creature.

3

I've been a whole zoo, you know. Everything from a fly to an elephant. Bat. Owl. I've flown, way up in the sky with eagle wings. I've flown up there with Tobias. Way up in the clouds. If there's something better than that, well, I never found it.

It's not magic. Just technology. Of course technology always seems like magic at first. Haul a tenth-century knight into the modern age and show him your cell phone or your TV or your computer or your car. Magic.

This technology came from the Andalites. The Andalites are enemies of the Yeerks, and I guess allies of ours, though right at the moment they were more likely to annihilate Earth than the Yeerks were. You know the old saying, "With friends like these, who needs enemies?"

Anyway, it began with a chance meeting. An Andalite prince named Elfangor crashed his shot-up fighter in our path. Coincidence? No, history. And a helping hand from the Ellimist who of course never lends a helping hand.

Elfangor died, but not before he told us what was happening and gave us the morphing technology.

I've been a rat. A dolphin . . . oh, man, do they have fun. That rush when you're zooming straight up through the water, when you see the ripply surface of the sea, when you blow through that barrier and soar through the air . . . And then, splash! And do it all over again.

So, anyway, we decided we had to try and stop the Yeerks. Jake and Tobias and Cassie and Marco and Ax, who is Elfangor's little brother, and me. We lived this secret life. We fought and mostly lost, but we survived. We frustrated the Yeerks. We ruined Visser Three's life, though he still managed to be promoted to Visser One.

Maybe we did too good a job frustrating the visser. The Yeerks grew tired of infiltration. Visser One had been craving open war. And when we blew up their ground-based Yeerk pool, the source of their food, the center of their lives, it was gloves off.

So much the better as far as I was concerned. The time had come to settle things.

The Yeerks obliterated our town to create a dead zone around their construction of a new Yeerk pool. They were in a hurry. Without a functioning pool they were getting hungry.

But there was a worm gnawing at the Yeerk race. They had acquired morphing technology themselves — in part because of what Jake thought was Cassie's betrayal.

Cassie sees further than I do. Further than any of us. She sees deep. The girl cannot dress or accessorize to save her life, she's a girl who wears manure-stained Wal-Mart jeans for crying out loud, but Cassie sees connections and possibilities that others don't.

She let Tom take the morphing cube. And that changed everything. Some Yeerks began to see a way out of their parasitic lives. The hunger-crazed Taxxons — a race held captive by the Yeerks — began to dream of a life without their Yeerk overlords. A revolution was brewing.

At the same time, the Andalite fleet was closing in, ready to obliterate Earth as the only way to stop the Yeerk infestation. They had watched the Yeerks concentrate their forces on Earth. They were ready to bring down the curtain: Obliterate Earth and the Yeerk Empire would be gutted.

Too bad about those creatures who got in the way. What were they called? Oh yeah, humans.

But Tom betrayed his visser, betrayed the Yeerk race. Not for the sake of poor old humanity, but for his own ambition. He would escape with the morphing cube and with a hard core of faithful Yeerk supporters. He would abandon the Yeerk people to the Andalite vengeance, destroy the hated Animorphs, and if H. sapiens was annihilated, too, well . . .

That's where Jake saw his chance. Tom's Yeerk is smart. Jake is smarter.

Now Jake and the others had control of the

Yeerk Pool ship. Tom had control of the visser's own personal Blade ship.

Tom — the Yeerk in Tom's head — was closing in for his final act of betrayal: He would kill his master, Visser One, and doom his fellow Yeerks. He thought we were already dead.

Surprise, Tom.

My favorite morph was the grizzly bear. Seven feet tall standing erect. You cannot imagine the power, especially when united with human intelligence and knowledge. Compared to my grizzly morph a human being is like something made out of glued-together Popsicle sticks.

How many times have I felt that change as muscle piles on muscle, as the thick brown fur covers me, as the rail spike claws grow from my fingers?

The grizzly bear and I had been through a lot together.

I would go to grizzly to kill Tom.

CHAPTER 2

I was a flea on Tom's head. A flea can't see much really, just an impression of light or dark. Not my favorite morph. But if you want to hide out, unnoticed, on a human body, you can't beat the flea. And with practice you can learn to understand speech from the distant, distorted vibrations that reach your quivering antennae.

My time was coming, and I had to find a place to demorph and remorph. I fired the spring-loaded legs and catapulted into the air.

It took forever for me to fall. The first time you do it it scares the pee out of you. Falling and falling like that. Like you jumped off the moon and were falling to Earth.

8

I hit the deck, a fall of thousands of times my own height. Flea didn't care. Not even a bruise.

A strained voice said, "That's . . . that's not a waste dump. They aren't dumping waste! That's the pool. The main pool. It's been flushed."

There was an audible gasp from several voices. The human-Controllers and Hork-Bajir-Controllers who were Tom's bridge crew.

"Sensors showing . . . it's our people. Sixteen thousand . . . maybe seventeen thousand."

Tom cut in harshly. "It saves us the trouble of killing them ourselves." Then, in an undertone, "But why? Why would the visser flush . . . what does this mean?"

It means Jake's alive, Tommy boy. You'll fig-ure it out in a minute, Yeerk. But I'm guessing it will be too late.

Away from blood. That's where I had to go. The flea's senses were all attuned to the warm scent of blood. But that scent represented dan-ger to me now, and I hopped away, each bound-ing leap the equivalent of a human jumping over the Grand Canyon. Try getting a flea morph to move *away* from blood. Amazing how much resis-tance you can get from a brain that's about ten cells big.

I felt shade. Absence of light. Distance from vibration. No scent of blood.

9

Was I in a safe place? Surely not, but maybe safe enough.

I began a slow, cautious demorph.

I heard a yell.

"The Pool ship is preparing to fire!"

"Hard left!" Tom yelled.

A moment later, Tom laughed. "The visser's lost maneuvering ability. The Pool ship handles like a drunken Gedd at the best of times, and now look at it."

Someone else reported, "His Dracon cannon is powering down. I show his reserves at less than ten percent."

"Are they? Well, well," Tom said. "Hail the visser. On screen."

I was halfway demorphed. I was a hideous creature made up of armored plates and prickly legs and human flesh spreading across me like a wave. The sickest imagination could not conjure up the true creepiness of a half-flea human. Human eyes, my own eyes, bulged from an insect face.

I could see. Not well, confused, distorted, my visual cortex still more flea than human. I was still on the bridge of the Blade ship. I was actually crouched beneath an unoccupied control station. It was like hiding under a desk. Fortunately it was designed for a Hork-Bajir body, so there was some room.

I saw the viewscreen light up. I saw Visser One's Andalite face. It was different. There was a dull look in his usually aggressive eyes, a slackness in the normally tensed body.

"You seem to be experiencing some engine trouble, Visser," Tom gloated.

I was completely demorphed now. There would be no room for me to morph all the way to grizzly and stay concealed. Every eye on the bridge was watching the screen, but a seven-foot bear looming up will definitely attract attention.

I started the morph. If it turned out I wasn't needed, well, then it would be fatally stupid of me. But I had no real doubt.

Visser One said, <The Empire will track you down and kill you, you do understand that, I hope?>

"Oh, I doubt it. I think the Empire will have its hands full," Tom said cheerfully. "The Andalite fleet is rather close by. It's possible that I misled you on that point."

He was all but giggling.

Then, the viewscreen widened out and he saw, and I saw, the lithe Bengal tiger standing near the visser.

Tobias was there, too.

Tom saw the tiger and knew it was Jake and knew in that split second that he had been outmaneuvered, outfought. He took a step back, like he'd been punched. "You're not dead!" he cried.

<I noticed the same thing,> Visser One said dryly.

Tom yelled, "Bring us around to target the Pool ship's bridge. Do it! Now! Now! Bring us around!"

At that moment I could have morphed all the way to elephant without being noticed. Tom's panic was infectious. They all knew they'd been had.

But they didn't know how. Tom's reaction was pure instinct: shoot. He'd forgotten that the Pool ship was helpless. The sight of Jake — who should be dead — standing there with the other Animorphs, standing there alive and apparently in control of the Pool ship . . . all Tom could think of was shooting.

The danger was closer than that.

Jake looked at me. Like he knew I was watching him.

<Rachel,> he said. <Go.>

<Rachel . . .> Tobias said.

<I know, Tobias. I know.> I said.

I was still not completely morphed when someone shrieked. "Animorph!"

After all these years of the Yeerks thinking we were Andalites, always yelling "Andalite!" whenever they saw a morph. It was strangely gratifying that at last they knew who we were.

I said, <That's right, genius: Animorph.>

I did what I do better than anyone. What Jake counted on me to do.

I attacked.

CHAPTER 3

I charged straight for Tom, on all fours, head down, an express train of muscle and fur, claws and teeth.

I hit him with my lowered head and knocked him back into the viewscreen. Not enough to take Tom out, but I had to try and damage the ship.

Tseeew!

Someone fired a Dracon beam. I felt the searing pain in my right flank but it didn't matter. I was in berserk mode. Pain was something that could be stored up for later. Right now I was an enraged bear. I slammed a shoulder left, slammed a shoulder right and felt crumpling metal.

Tom yelled, "No shooting! You'll destroy the bridge! Morph! Morph you idiots!"

I swung a paw at him, and it should have been all over right then, but I missed. He dropped and I missed.

I reared up to my full height and Tom rolled into a ball. He was down under my legs. I swiped his back and laid his spine open. But I didn't stop him.

He was through my legs and behind me and staggering toward the exit.

I spun, dropped to all fours and bounded to cut him off. I reached the exit a split second before him and shouldered him aside in the process. He spun like a top and fell on his butt.

I was in a clumsy stance so I just sort of dropped on him. It was like some WWF body slam, only I wasn't faking it. He grunted and I saw blood gush from his nose and mouth.

Too easy. My final battle. It couldn't be this easy.

I drew back, ready to go in and finish the job. But I had wasted too much time. There were others on the bridge. And I had overlooked the fact that we were no longer the only ones who could morph. Every member of Tom's handpicked crew could morph, and I was surrounded now by a half dozen half-morphed beasts.

Tom himself was starting to morph, but he wasn't my main problem now.

<Rachel! Behind!>

It was Jake. He was watching the fight from the Pool ship.

I spun, slashed horizontally and something that may have been a half-morphed leopard crumpled like a Dixie cup.

The main weapons station was right there, a sort of waist-high, freestanding lectern. I threw myself back into it and heard a nice crunch as it toppled.

But that was more seconds lost while the Yeerks were completing their morphs. All but Tom. His scarred back was crusting over with reptilian scales, but he was nothing recognizable yet. And in any case, I had plenty to keep me busy.

I faced two lionesses, a cape buffalo, and a polar bear. It was a whole zoo full of dangerous animals. The polar bear was my equal all by himself. The cape buffalo maybe as well. I could take either lioness, but the combination was going to be rough.

For a wondrous, frozen moment we all waited, stared, breathed, tensed, expectant.

I felt . . .

I felt exalted.

It was my moment. This was my place and my time and my own perfection.

I was no longer afraid. Weird. If I'd had a mouth I'd have smiled.

<Well?> I said.

No one moved.

<Scared?> I asked.

No answer.

<You should be,> I said, almost laughing.

I lunged, straight for the polar bear. Go for the main opponent first. Go for the danger. I barreled straight into him. It was a train crash. I slammed him, my shoulder into the side of his head.

He *had* a bear morph. I *was* my bear morph. Experience is very helpful.

The polar bear staggered. I extended my claws and in a move no real bear had ever learned, I drove them straight into him, like four daggers, right beneath the front right shoulder: the heart. I hit him again before the cape buffalo slammed me and knocked me, windless, rolling into the bulkhead.

The buffalo backed up and came at me again, the wide, thick horns like a battering ram. But the beast's hooves were designed for dirt and grass, not the slippery floor. He didn't fall but he lost a lot of speed and momentum. He hit me in my exposed belly. It would have killed me if he'd been up to speed. Even so it crushed the last ounce of air from my lungs. I felt like someone had dropped a house on me.

A lioness was on my face, clawing madly, like a crazed alley cat. The other one was trying to bite my neck — a waste of time. No one bites through a grizzly's fur.

I was down, buried under mad fur. I was down, slashed at, punched, hammered, clawed. My legs were in the air, helpless!

I drew my legs close and shifted my weight. Got my legs under me. I lifted myself and the two lions. I shook myself violently and threw off the lion who'd been on my face. I aimed a blow at her but she was too fast.

Out of the corner of my eye I saw the polar bear demorphing. It's the only way when your morph body is dying: demorph and fast. Die in morph and you're dead. Period.

But I was missing something. Something nagged at me.

<Tom!> Jake yelled. <Tom!>

The cape buffalo butted me in the hindquarters and spun me around. The lion on my back was reaching around like it was trying to strangle me, digging busy claws into the folds of loose skin around my throat.

The second lion charged gamely, leaped and sank its teeth into my left haunch.

Had to take down the Yeerk with the polar bear morph. Had to stop him remorphing. I'd been lucky once, experience had told. But I couldn't count on a second easy win against a polar bear.

I tried to stagger forward, but the buffalo had done some damage now. My hindquarters were numb and weak. He was hitting me with short, sharp blows, like a boxer rabbit-punching. He'd figured out that he couldn't really wind up and deliver a killing blow.

<Tom! Rachel, Tom! Look out for Tom!>

Jake's voice was far away. Strange.

The slick floor that handicapped the buffalo now worked against me, too. I couldn't get enough traction with my blood-slicked pads.

Had to get the Yeerk with the polar bear morph. He was demorphed now. Ready to start morphing and come back rejuvenated.

So heavy. Floor all covered in blood. Wow, they were really bleeding.

My front right leg suddenly buckled. It was a pail of ice water in my face, a sudden realization.

My blood. That was my blood on the floor.

White fur began to ripple across the morphing Yeerk.

<He's a snake!> a voice cried. <Rachel!>

No, he's a bear, I thought.

A flash of movement, so fast it was a blur. Something in my eyes! Burning. I couldn't see. That's okay, okay, bears can't see all that well anyway, I had . . . I had . . .

A cobra, some distant, strange, analytical

19

part of my brain noted. Tom's morph: a cobra. The venom was in my eyes.

I couldn't think. Couldn't see.

Demorph.

No. Bear. The lions on me.

Weak. Strange to be the bear and be weak. Strange.

I realized I was no longer standing. I was flat on the floor. I heard my own slow breathing. I should be panting.

Something striking at my face again and again. The cobra. Couldn't even see him.

I had failed. Tom. Alive.

<Die, human,> he said. <Just die.>

<Rachel!> Tobias cried.

<Help me, Tobias,> I pleaded.

<I can't . . . I . . .>

He didn't understand. <Help me get him. Help me get him!>

<Okay. Okay. He's . . . your left paw, toward your face. Get ready. Has to be fast.>

<I'm ready.>

<Now!>

I jerked my paw, claws extended toward my face.

Tom shrieked. I couldn't see him. But I felt something squirming. Like a worm on a fishhook. The snake was impaled on my claws.

<No!> Tom cried in outrage.

I brought my paw to my mouth.

<Sorry,> I said vaguely.

<Jake, stop her!> the Yeerk screamed with Tom's mouth.

I bit down on the snake.

CHAPTER 4

I lay there in suspended animation.

I felt myself floating.

The bear was melting. Old grizzly bear, my friend. Good old bear.

I demorphed. The snake was still in my mouth. Motionless.

I demorphed.

I was Rachel again, the human Rachel, alive, unhurt. I could have bounded up and gone off to the mall to shop. But I didn't kid myself. I didn't hope.

I spit the snake out.

I was surrounded on all sides. I was only a weak human girl now. The polar bear loomed over me, his strength the equal of my own grizzly, but now I was just me, just Rachel.

I could see the viewscreen. I could see my best friend Cassie. Jake. Marco, funny Marco. Ax.

Tobias.

He had morphed. He was his human self once more. He'd done that for me. And because he was crying. I understood. Humans cry, hawks don't.

"I love you," I said to the screen.

And oh, god, how could so much regret and so much sweetness and so much sadness all be present in that single moment. I was already dead and missing my unlived life. I was already dead and Tobias was mourning.

I tried to smile. For him.

The polar bear said, <You fight well, human.>

Then he killed me with a single blow.

Time stopped.

He came to me. The Ellimist.

The puppet master come to watch my final act. It figured. He was in his saintly old man guise. As fake as everything else about him. The all-powerful weakling. The mighty manipulator.

"You," I said accusingly.

"Yes."

"Who are you?" I demanded. "Who are you to play games with us? You appear, you disappear, you use us, who are you, what are you?"

And then, for what seemed a very long time, the Ellimist told me. I saw. I understood.

But I also knew he would not save me. That he couldn't under the arcane rules of his millennia-long war with Crayak.

The Ellimist was there to honor me, and I guess that was nice of him. Wasn't going to help me much.

I wanted so much to live. I wanted so much to stay and not to leave. In a moment no answer would matter to me, but just the same, I wanted to know what I guess any dying person wants to know.

"Answer this, Ellimist: Did I . . . did I make a difference? My life, and my . . . my death . . . was I worth it? Did my life really matter?"

"Yes," he said. "You were brave. You were strong. You were good. You mattered."

"Yeah. Okay, then. Okay, then."

I wondered if —

CHAPTER 5

Jake

No one moved.

I don't think anyone even breathed.

Toby, the leader of the free Hork-Bajir, burst onto the bridge. She was scarred and bloody. <Jake, they're surrendering. We had to promise them amnesty and a chance to acquire the morphing power.>

I heard her words.

<What's the matter?> Toby asked.

She noticed Tobias. She'd only seen him in human morph a few times. Toby is named for Tobias. The free Hork-Bajir see Tobias as their liberator. And Toby, the Hork-Bajir seer, was named in his honor.

On the screen I saw the Blade ship slowly picking up speed and pulling away. They didn't fire at us.

Tom was dead.

And I wondered how I was ever going to explain it. I had ordered my cousin to execute my brother. How would I ever explain that?

All these years I'd fought to keep us all alive, to stop the Yeerks, always with the hope that someday I would save my brother, that he would come back, that he'd be Tom again. That was why I'd enlisted in the war to begin with. I was going to save Tom.

Tom was dead. The Yeerk in his head was dead.

And Rachel.

And how many others?

General Doubleday's soldiers who had provided the suicidal diversionary attack on the ground.

The auxiliary Animorphs who had gone with them to trick the enemy.

How many of Toby's people?

Seventeen thousand Yeerks, frozen. Flushed into space.

Plus.

Plus.

All at my command.

<Jake, I need your okay,> Toby pressed. <The Yeerks want you. They want your assurance.>

<A pack of traitors,> Visser One said, but the fight had gone out of him.

Tom was dead. Rachel was dead. How would I explain this to my parents?

Silly to think of that right then. Silly and stupid.

<Jake . . .> Toby urged.

<Rachel,> Cassie said softly. <Toby, we lost Rachel. And Tom is dead.>

Toby absorbed that, then said, <Jara Hamee, my father, died bravely in battle here today.>

Still I couldn't say anything. How did I explain . . .

Marco was still in gorilla morph. He said, <It's okay, Toby. Tell the Yeerks that Jake will be along in a minute. Tell them Visser One is our captive. Tell them we approve the deal you made.>

<My people may not agree,> Ax said.

<Yeah?> Marco shot back. <Guess what? This is *our* planet. These are *our* prisoners. This is *our* victory. If the Andalite high command doesn't like it they can come and try to take a piece of us.>

Cassie came to me and sort of leaned into me, as close to a hug as we could get right then. I was afraid she would say something sympathetic, I was afraid she would comfort me, and if

27

she had I think that would have been it, I think
my brain would have just shut down because all
the pain would have suddenly been real and
deep inside me.

Cassie said, <We still need you. You're not
done yet, Jake.>

The right thing to say. Cassie was good at
that. I noted the effect on me, observed my reaction from a million miles away.

I sighed. Okay. Yeah. I still had a job. Do the
job.

<Everything else can wait,> Cassie said.

Yeah. It could all wait.

I took a deep breath.

<Okay, Toby. Okay, I'll be right there. Tell
them what Marco said and I'll get there soon to
back you up.>

Toby left with a last, curious glance at Tobias.
Me, I couldn't look at Tobias. I didn't care if he
saw the way I avoided his eyes, I didn't care, I
couldn't look at him.

I wish to god Tobias had just come after me.
Right then. I would have welcomed it.

Instead I focused on Visser One. How had this
happened? How had he survived and Tom died?
How did he still live? How could that be the result?

<I imagine it's time to kill me,> Visser One
said. <You'll be doing me a favor. Whatever death

28

you have for me will be nothing compared to what the Council of Thirteen would sentence me to. They really don't approve of vissers who lose Pool ships.>

<No. No more killing,> I said.

"What do you mean, no more killing?" Tobias demanded, breaking his ringing silence at last. He stabbed a finger at the visser. "He's the one responsible for all this!"

<He's a prisoner of war,> I said softly. <We don't kill prisoners.>

<No, of course not,> Visser One mocked. <You merely destroy the ground-based Yeerk pool and kill thousands. And you add another seventeen thousand here on this ship. All defenseless, unhosted Yeerks. But you don't kill prisoners.>

<Marco?>

<Yeah, Jake.>

<The visser is going to remove himself from this Andalite body he has stolen and inhabited for so long. Find a safe place for him. Watch over him.>

<You got it.>

<Cassie? Go get Erek. If he wants the Chee secret to be kept he needs to hide himself. We may have guests soon.>

<Anything else?> Cassie asked.

<Like what?> I snapped. <An apology? To that robot? "Sorry we blackmailed you into help-

ing us?" No. He drained off the Dracon beams and because of that the Blade ship got away. Because of that Rachel died in vain. Because of him who knows what will happen?>

Cassie hesitated, looked down, then turned to go.

I began to demorph, then stopped myself. The visser was still a dangerous foe with a bottomless grab bag of powerful morphs at his command.

I spoke to Ax in private thought-speak. His tail blade flashed and caught the visser unprepared, a flat-side smack against his temple. His host body, the long-enslaved Andalite war prince called Alloran, slumped unconscious.

<I know you can still hear me in there, Visser. I'll make this simple: You exit that body. You do it right now because if you don't we're going to cut our way in and yank you out.>

<Tobias? Marco? Find a box, a jar, something to hold this Yeerk in when he emerges. If he doesn't come out within two minutes, do it the hard way.>

<That would be my pleasure,> Marco said.

<Okay, Ax,> I said. <Dial up the Andalite high command. Tell them to stand by for a communication from me. And open a simultaneous channel directly to the Andalite home world.>

Ax hesitated. He turned his main eyes to me even as his stalk eyes remained focused on the visser. <*Prince* Jake, there is a specific regulation forbidding me as an *aristh* from contacting the civilian media net. I am required to work through the chain of command, my *prince*.>

He wasn't fighting me, just asking for dispensation. The repetition of the word *prince* signaled his willingness.

I began to demorph, moving from tiger to human, from thought-speak to spoken word. <Ax, as your prince I'm ordering you to ignore those regulations and do what I've told you to do.>

<Then I must obey.>

"Yeah. Now, I have to go see about Toby and then I'll be back. I want to see one slug in a jar and a ticked-off Andalite on screen when I get back."

I left the bridge, trotted to catch up with Toby and followed her to engineering where the signs of a severe battle were evident. Hork-Bajir bodies were stacked in the corridor. Their blood was everywhere. Impossible to be sure which were free Hork-Bajir, our allies, and which had died still enslaved to the Yeerks.

Toby's people controlled the doorway into engineering where the dispirited Yeerks had taken refuge.

31

"Do they have a spokesman?" I asked.

Toby yelled, "Sub-Visser Seventy-four, the Animorph leader Jake is here."

A battered-looking Hork-Bajir female stepped into view. I looked her up and down, putting on my hard act. "We have the ship. We have Visser One. You're not in much of a position to make demands."

The sub-visser showed nothing. "Human, you cannot frighten us. We have no hope left and that gives us strength. We will not die of Kandrona starvation — better to die here, now, in battle. We'll kill some more of your people before we do."

I nodded. "Fair enough. You want amnesty, access to Kandrona rays, and morphing technology? You'd accept permanent morphing and relocation?"

"As opposed to slow death by starvation or even a quick death now? Yes."

"I don't have the morphing cube. But I pledge to use all my influence to gain agreement from the Andalites when they come."

She stood there, straight, almost at attention for a while, then slumped. "It has come to this after all."

I nodded. "Yeah. The onboard Yeerk pool needs to be refilled. Send some of your people under Toby's supervision to handle that. Then you'll be escorted to the pool in groups of six. You'll exit your host bodies."

"And be helpless again," the Yeerk said bitterly.

"I keep my word," I said.

I started to leave then stopped. "Toby? I'm sorry about Jara Hamee. He was . . ."

"He was the first of the free Hork-Bajir," Toby said fiercely. "He was the father of his people. And he was *my* father."

I started back for the bridge.

CHAPTER 6

Cassie

Rachel dead? How could that be? How could that be real?

She'd been my best friend forever. Teased me about my clothes as I teased her about her obsessive shopping. How long ago had that been? A hundred years?

She'd wanted to be a gymnast but thought she was probably too tall ever to be really good. And of course all that was in the past, too.

She had this way of seeming untouched by what went on around her. Unaffected. Above. She was a person who could walk through a car wash and come out dry. She could move through a mosh pit and never be jostled. She could wear a white dress to dig in the mud and somehow never get a spot on her.

But the war had touched her. She'd changed, and she'd known she was changing. The war had revealed a hidden part of her soul. She alone, of all of us, she alone liked it. Loved it, even. She had enjoyed the fight.

Sometimes I imagined her as a Viking. Or as a knight on a quest. That's what she was: a joyful warrior.

And she had died fighting against impossible odds.

Like a hole inside me. Like someone had taken a knife and carved a hole in my chest. Like I might cave in, be swallowed up and disappear in that hole.

Beautiful Rachel.

Poor Tom.

And now, all of us, the survivors. The victim-perpetrators.

I found Erek. I simply walked through the Yeerk ship calling out in thought-speak. A wolf prowling strangely empty, silent corridors.

He appeared before me. He's an android, one of a long-lived species called the Chee. Their creators, the Pemalites, are extinct, but the pacific instincts of the Pemalites live on in these magnificent thinking machines.

35

Erek is at least five thousand years old, and the person we knew by that name was really just a holographic projection that disguised the machine beneath the illusion.

I demorphed.

"Hi, Erek."

"Hi, Cassie." He smiled sadly. "Jake sent you."

I nodded.

"I see. He feels guilty."

"No. Not guilty."

His eyes narrowed. "Then what? He used me, blackmailed me, manipulated my programming to get me to break through the security grid and take control of this ship."

"You drained the Dracon beams."

"What did Jake expect me to do? I had given him control when he needed it. I wasn't going to enable him to kill."

"The Blade ship got away. Rachel . . . Jake had Rachel with Tom. Rachel and Tom are both . . . and the ship got away anyway. Thanks to you."

The Erek hologram disappeared. He was an android now, a thing of steel and ivory vaguely in the shape of a dog walking erect. "And I'm supposed to feel regret because Jake ordered his cousin to kill his brother and I didn't allow him to massacre everyone else on the Blade ship?"

That made me mad and I guess I showed it.

"So, you, too, huh Cassie?"

"Jake did what he had to do."

"Did he? Someone flushed the Yeerk pool into space. Did he have to do that, too? They were un-hosted Yeerks. They were harmless."

"We needed a div —" I stopped myself.

"A what? A what did you need? A diversion? You're going to tell me you needed a diversion so Jake massacred seventeen thousand sentient creatures? A diversion?"

I took a deep breath. "Jake says maybe you should get off the ship, Erek. The Andalites will most likely be coming aboard soon. It's up to you whether you go on keeping your existence secret. We won't divulge it."

"I see."

"Bye Erek."

He nodded. Then, as he was passing, he took my arm in his pseudo-hand. "Take care of Jake. He's going to need you."

CHAPTER 7

Marco

Ax and I watched fascinated, repulsed, maybe a little triumphant, as the Yeerk crawled slowly from the Andalite ear.

I had found a lockable briefcase, a very human artifact stuffed under a control panel. It was filled with chocolate chip cookies. Some Yeerk, probably a human-Controller, had developed a sweet tooth and it would be hard to get a good cookie on a Yeerk ship.

I ate a cookie and held the case open for the slug-like creature that was the true Visser One.

<I could easily cut him in half,> Ax said conversationally.

<Yeah, well, better not, I guess.>

Tobias had returned to what was his normal

form. The red-tailed hawk perched on a railing. The laser eyes drilled into the Yeerk. I was not at all sure that Tobias wouldn't swoop over and nail the visser. I wasn't at all sure I'd stop him.

I'm probably the least emotional of the group. It's always been my virtue and my failing that I see the clear path from A to Z without the distraction of moral considerations. I don't want to say I'm ruthless, I'm not. But I have the ability. I can see the ruthless way clearly. I have to sort of add the morality back into the equation after the fact.

I had no deep qualms about the seventeen thousand, any more than I had about our attack on the ground-based Yeerk pool. I knew why Jake had sent Rachel to Tom. I agreed with his thinking. But then, I wasn't in love with Rachel. I wasn't some lonely kid trapped in a hawk's body, half in one world, half in another with only Rachel's love tying me to my humanity.

Maybe Tobias would eventually accept what Jake did. Maybe not.

It was weird. I was watching our greatest foe place himself literally into our hands. We had beaten Visser One.

Maybe later we'd celebrate.

"Ax, pick him up."

Ax picked up the Yeerk holding him between two fingers, gingerly, as though it was something dirty.

39

He dropped it into the briefcase. I closed the lid and turned the combo lock.

"I guess we won, Ax."

<Yes.>

"Shouldn't someone be singing 'God Bless America'?"

Ax looked puzzled and decided to let it go. He said, <I must access the communications array and carry out Jake's orders.>

The remaining Yeerks on the bridge were being very cooperative now. Seeing your great leader in a box will do that, I guess. Anyway, they followed Ax's instructions.

It took a few minutes and then, on the screen there appeared a wary Andalite face.

<What do you want, Yeerk?>

Ax said, <We are not Yeerks. I am *aristh* Aximili-Esgarrouth-Isthill, the brother of Prince Elfangor. You have correctly identified this signal as originating from a Yeerk pool ship, but this ship is now under the control of . . .> He frowned, uncertain, and turned a quizzical stalk eye to me.

I shrugged. "This ship is under the control of the Earth Liberation Army." I grinned. It was a wonderfully grandiose name for a handful of kids.

Ax repeated it word for word to the skeptical Andalite.

<Do you seriously expect to me to believe that humans have seized control of a Yeerk Pool ship, *aristh* Aximili-Esgarrouth-Isthill? Clearly you are a Controller. Just as clearly this is a clumsy trap.>

Cassie returned. She took in the scene and decided to stay quiet.

"He's got us there," I admitted. "He has no way of knowing whether we're really us or Controllers."

Ax said, <There is a Yeerk Blade ship heading . . .> He consulted a display panel and gave the coordinates. <You may be able to intercept them.>

The Andalite officer said, <Anything else, Yeerk? Is there another part to this pitiful attempt at a trap?> He was about to sign off.

Jake arrived. "Where do we stand?" he asked me.

I motioned at the screen. "This genius thinks we're Controllers trying to set him up."

Jake nodded. "Perfect," he said dryly. "How do we get around this?"

<Tell him you'll surrender the Pool ship to them.>

It was Visser One! No. No, it was the Andalite Visser One had infested for so many, many years: Alloran-Semitur-Corrass. I'd forgotten all about

41

him. Ax had knocked him unconscious, now he was coming around. He climbed to his hooves, looking like a stunned blue deer.

The Andalite officer said, <So the deception is over. I see the visser has revealed himself.>

Alloran started to say something, then turned his face and main eyes to Jake. <With your permission?>

That was one weird moment. Alloran was an arrogant, determined, even criminally ruthless Andalite war prince. Or had been once, long ago. And then, for a long time, that face had been the face of our deadliest enemy, Visser Three/One. And now he was meekly waiting for Jake's okay.

Jake nodded and in a very respectful tone said, "Please continue, War-Prince Alloran."

Alloran's main eyes flickered, a slight display of emotion. <Who are you?> he demanded of the Andalite officer.

<I am Offeran-Jibril-Castant. I am officer of the day aboard the Andalite Dome ship . . .> He hesitated and there was a slight, ironic smile. An Andalite smile, of course, which is all in the eyes. <The Dome ship *Elfangor*.>

Ax swelled about a size. <A Dome ship named for Elfangor. There is no higher honor for a warrior.>

<A well-named ship,> Alloran said. <Now,

officer-of-the-day Offeran, you're going to want to contact the captain because you have just captured a Yeerk Pool ship. We will advance at space normal speed to any point you name. All Bug fighters will be deployed around the ship, and as we reach the rendezvous point you will see all Bug fighters self-destruct. At that time we will detach the Pool ship's main engines. All weapons will be powered down. This ship will be perfectly helpless.>

That got Offeran's attention. He turned a shade of lighter blue. It was kind of as if in the middle of World War II the Japanese Navy had called up the U.S. Navy and said, "Hey, we're going to turn over our biggest aircraft carrier to you. Come on over and pick up the keys."

Suddenly the scene changed. The face on the screen was older. This Andalite had a burn scar on his scalp and was missing one stalk eye.

<Captain-Prince Asculan-Semitur-Langor,> Ax said in private thought-speak.

"Big time?" I whispered under my breath.

<*Very* big time.>

The captain favored us with a long, hard, serious look. Then he said, <Visser, I refuse to —>

I saw it coming. The old Andalite was going to chill us. It wasn't my place to butt in, maybe, but I couldn't let this old creep screw everything up by committing himself. Once he said what he was getting ready to say it would be impossible for him to climb down.

"Hey, Ax-man," I said brightly. "Is it true the Andalite home world is watching all this? Can I wave to them?" I waved like one of the idiots outside the *Today* show. "Hi, everyone! Howard Stern rules! Yaaaah!"

Well, that stopped everyone and everything dead. You could practically see the wheels turning in old Asculan's nasty-looking head. Jake looked for a minute like he might slap me silly. And Ax basically turned to stone.

But then Jake gave me a nod. He got it.

So did Alloran. <I should have mentioned that under orders from his prince, *aristh* Aximili has patched this communication through to the civilian net.>

Asculan had a mean look to him now. Furious. He was a person in a trap. A powerful person in a trap, not used to being trapped, not liking it.

Jake stepped into Asculan's line of sight. "Captain Asculan, we know that the Andalite fleet is devoted to the destruction of the Yeerk threat. And we know that you must be personally committed to that goal."

I translated in my head: *We know you've come here to turn Earth into a great big charcoal briquette because you think it's the only way to stop the Yeerks.*

"Because of your devotion to duty it may almost seem a disappointment to reach your goal at long last, only to discover that your foe has essentially surrendered."

Translation: *It's over.*

"At this point we have to set aside the necessary ruthlessness of war, the suspicion and hostility, and turn instead to the more satisfying duties of making peace."

Translation: *Your people back home are watching and if you come in guns blazing, annihilating a peaceful people, your own peaceful civilians will never stand for it.*

"Our victory could never have occurred without the support of our Andalite friends."

Translation: *Look, we're willing to share the credit. You people did squat for us, but we're willing to spread the kudos around freely.*

"I look forward to our two peaceful peoples working closely together, to forming a deep and abiding friendship. We have so much to learn from our Andalite brothers, just as we have already learned so much from the great Elfangor and his no less courageous and resourceful brother, Aximili."

Translation: *The Dome ship* Elfangor *is going*

to come in and annihilate all of the real Elfangor's work? Kill his little brother who happens to be a ready-made Andalite hero? Guess again, you mean old fart.

The captain listened to all this impassively. But I could see the steam sort of leaking out of him. By the end of Jake's little speech his eyes were glazed over. He knew he'd been trapped but good, and the truth was, he was probably relieved.

<Who *exactly* are you?> Asculan asked Jake.

I jerked a thumb at my friend. "This is Jake. Jake Berenson. President of Earth."

CHAPTER 8

Jake

We flew the Pool ship to a rendezvous point just beyond the moon's orbit. As we'd promised, we deployed the Bug fighters by remote control and blew them up. We detached the ship's engines and waited. Waited for hours.

Then, in a rush, perhaps two dozen of the slightly goofy-looking Andalite fighters came swooping around us. They surrounded us, shredder weapons aimed. It was a hair-raising moment.

Then the Dome ship *Elfangor* and another Dome ship came in from different directions. Dome ships are very cool and typically Andalite. They're built a little like palm trees. There's a

47

long trunk with engines at one end and a bulge for weapons and living quarters in the middle. On top you have a big glass dome over grass and trees and even streams and little hills. The Andalites are a grazing species: They love an open meadow.

Dome ships are also exceedingly well armed. I don't know who wins a straight-up fight between a Yeerk Pool ship and an Andalite Dome ship. But I know who wins when the Pool ship is disarmed and without engines.

The Andalites ran sensor probes and satisfied themselves that we were powered down and that no other Yeerk ships were in the immediate vicinity.

Asculan arrived soon after by shuttle, along with a half dozen tough-looking Andalite marines and as many officers. I sent Ax to meet them at the space dock. I waited on the bridge. Marco had insisted, saying that I had to play the part of the big boss.

"The boss doesn't go down to the airport, he sends a limo or whatever. The boss waits in headquarters."

"Is that so?" I said.

"Yeah. Look, Jake, you're a sixteen-year-old kid. But the Andalites don't know that, right? Play the part. *Be* the part." He laughed.

Tobias sent him a murderous look that stalled the laughter.

Very quietly Cassie said, "Tobias, this is a big moment. Don't you think Rachel would want us to enjoy it as much as we can?"

<I don't know,> he snapped. <If she were alive I'd ask her.>

The Andalite contingent swept onto the bridge. They were playing their own roles: The warriors very intimidating, fanning out to keep everyone covered, the captain himself moving with self-conscious dignity.

The junior officers must have been mostly technical types because they looked around like starving men at the big brunch buffet. They couldn't stop themselves from touching the Yeerk display panels and controls with greedy fingers. They exchanged giddy looks that said, "Can you believe we're on a Yeerk Pool ship?"

All of them, including the warriors, kept stealing looks at Alloran. He had been infamous even before being made into the first and only Andalite-Controller.

I took a deep breath and said, "Captain, thanks for coming over. As soon as we can settle some details, I'll be glad to turn this ship over to you."

<Details?>

"Yes. The Yeerk prisoners of war have been promised the opportunity to be subjected to the morphing technology. So have a number of Taxxons down on the surface."

<Denied,> the captain said.

It took me aback. I hadn't expected a flat denial.

"I promised them."

<You had no right to promise what you do not own.>

I didn't want to get mad. Fortunately I had Marco to do that for me.

"Hey, we're handing you a Yeerk Pool ship. And by the way, there are another couple of dozen major Yeerk vessels back in orbit around Earth and you can snap them up easy. Thanks to us."

<We're very grateful,> Asculan said blandly, speaking to me and refusing to directly acknowledge Marco. <But Yeerk technology, while no doubt fascinating to my officers, is less sophisticated than our own. It is of interest, but no more than that.>

Marco erupted. "We won your lousy war for you, you pompous old —"

"My promise to the Yeerks and the Taxxons will be honored," I said, trying my best to sound determined and confident and forceful.

<The morphing technology is the property of

the Andalite people. I am aware that you are morph-capable yourself, as well as a number of your people. Despite the fact that this was illegal, we don't intend to take any action against you for that. But the technology will not be made available any further.>

Cassie said, "Sir, don't you understand? This is the way out. The Yeerks are parasites who require other bodies in order to see, to move about freely. As long as that's the case they'll be trouble. Maybe not for us or for the Andalites anymore, but for someone."

<Now you're proposing the technology be made freely available to the entire Yeerk species?> Asculan laughed derisively. <You can't be serious. This will never happen. No Yeerk, no Taxxon will ever be given the morphing technology. Am I clear?>

No one said anything. I was stunned. It was clear to me now: We had no way to convince the Andalite military. They had their "weapon," they were going to keep it. And if that meant the war continued, that was fine with them.

And what did I have that could make them change their minds? Nothing. With the Pool ship and its information in their possession they'd be able to destroy the remainder of the Yeerk fleet. As for the Taxxons on Earth and the remaining leaderless, cutoff, isolated Yeerks on Earth, that wasn't the Andalites' problem: They knew we'd deal with that.

Checkmate.

I was honestly tempted to surrender the point. We had won. Earth was saved. What did I care if the Taxxons on Earth were rounded up and killed? That's what would happen, there was no alternative, Taxxons could never be allowed to live on Earth. And what did I care for promises made to the Yeerks on board the Pool ship? I had tried to keep my promise. If I failed, so what?

Marco must have read my mind. He drifted up beside me and whispered in my ear. "We give in now, they own us."

As often was the case, Marco was seeing things I'd overlooked. He was right: The human race had just opened their first negotiation with an alien species with far superior technology. If this relationship started from an acceptance of Andalite superiority and human weakness it would always be that way. We'd end up being second-class citizens on our own planet.

But what was I supposed to do about that?

I looked at Tobias. Nothing. He was gone into his own world. Cassie could only look troubled. And Ax, well, Ax had done what he could, he had defied his own leaders, but he was, after all, an Andalite.

But, then, Ax said, <Captain-Prince Asculan, I hereby declare a challenge.>

A dozen Andalites stopped breathing.

I looked at Marco. He shrugged. He had no clue either.

Asculan laughed. <*Aristh*, you are not in a position to declare a challenge. You would have to be of princely rank or have the support of an Andalite of princely rank.>

Silence.

Then, <I hold that rank,> Alloran said.

A very long silence.

In a low, dangerous tone, Asculan said, <Alloran, you are under suspicion already for your actions on the Hork-Bajir world, I wouldn't —>

<What I did on the Hork-Bajir world was precisely what you and the fleet were preparing to do to *this* world,> Alloran shot back.

Asculan focused all his eyes forward, a sign of intense concentration for an Andalite. <I was under orders. *You* acted alone.>

<I still retain my rank,> Alloran grated. <I am a war prince. This *aristh* has declared a challenge and I support his challenge. The requirements of the law are satisfied.>

At that moment I think if someone had so much as sneezed there would have been a fight. Asculan's tail blade was twitching. He was ready to throw down.

But not all the Andalites shared his feeling. Some of the officers and even some of the warriors looked troubled. Troubled by their boss. Andalites take their laws seriously.

"Is someone going to maybe tell us what a challenge is?" Marco muttered.

It was Ax who answered. <It is the right and obligation of any Andalite warrior to challenge the order of a superior if he believes that superior is violating the fundamental rights of the electorate — the people.>

"You're kidding," Marco said. "How do you people ever fight wars if you can challenge anything your superior officer tells you to do?"

<If my challenge fails I will be harshly disciplined,> Ax said. <I will be exiled. Permanently. And my tail blade . . . My tail blade will be cut off.>

Alloran said, <Asculan, under the law you may declare an emergency and continue until we can arrange for the challenge to be judged at a later time. But I do not see how a court could agree that this negotiation over prisoners can possibly be called a legitimate emergency. In which case you would lose your rank and position and be exiled.>

<I know the law,> Asculan snapped.

I felt like a bystander at an event that would

determine the fate of the world. This was an all-Andalite show. Their law, their sense of right and wrong. I resented it. But I couldn't do anything but hope it would work out.

At last Asculan said, <I will confer with my officers.>

He seemed to think we should all leave the bridge and let him hold his meeting.

"I fought for this ship, Captain," I said. "You were invited aboard."

Probably not a good idea to antagonize the old monster, but I wasn't going to start playing the wimp now. We had paid for this ship. It was ours. If we gave it up it would be to allies, not overlords.

Asculan led his officers away. The rest of us let loose one very long sigh.

"What now?" I asked Ax.

He couldn't answer. He seemed to be shivering.

Alloran answered instead. <Asculan will contact the fleet high command. They will talk to their political advisors and try to decide whether they can win a challenge. It would be a sort of trial, with each side presenting evidence and witnesses. The entire Andalite electorate would have a vote. It would consume perhaps half a day.>

Marco said, "So what are the odds?"

Alloran shook his head. <I have been away from the home world a very long time. I do not know much about my people anymore. But the high command will make a cautious assessment. They are not bold or adventurous, they are more politicians than warriors. If Asculan comes back here prepared to go forward with the challenge, it will mean they are very, very confident of winning.>

"Okay. And by the way, Alloran, thanks for standing up for Ax. And all of us."

Alloran turned his main eyes to me. He gave me a strange look. <I never hoped to be free again. You freed me. I have done what I have done in my life. I am what I am, though I may have gained at least some wisdom through the years of enslavement to Visser One. Just the same, I will always be Alloran, the Butcher of Hork-Bajir. Alloran, the only Andalite to be taken alive by the Yeerks. But, disgraced, even despised, for whatever I am worth, I am yours to command.>

The speech was delivered in a low thought-speak tone, all emotion severely controlled. But then Alloran whipped his tail blade over his head, so fast it cracked like a whip. He smiled the subtle Andalite smile and yelled, <Do you

know who did that? Do you know who moved my tail? I did. I did. I did it.>

I smiled, but more for him than for me. If he would forever be the Butcher of Hork-Bajir, what would my name be?

Alloran's exuberance seemed to shake Ax out of his funk and he raised his own tail to touch the blade to Alloran's. <Welcome back, War-Prince Alloran.>

Asculan did not return to the bridge. He sent one of his junior officers, a calculated insult. But I guess no one really likes to admit face-to-face that they're beaten.

<Captain Asculan issues the following orders: Four morphing cubes will be made available to *aristh* Aximili to use as he sees fit. *Aristh* Aximili is hereby elevated to the rank of prince. Prince Aximili is appointed liaison between the Andalite fleet and the people of Earth.>

Asculan's officer waited, expecting a reply.

Ax said, <Thank the captain for me. I will carry out my duties to the best of my ability. My challenge is hereby withdrawn.>

And at that moment, with that polite exchange of messages, the war against the Yeerks was over.

CHAPTER 9

Cassie

Things happened quickly.

With terms now approved, the Yeerks on the Pool ship formalized their surrender.

The Pool ship joined the Andalite fleet in entering close Earth orbit where we contacted the remaining Yeerk ships and gave them the stark choice: Resist and die, or surrender and be transformed.

Some Yeerk ships contacted the Yeerk home world and received instructions to fight. But the Andalites had all the technical data of the Pool ship — including disabling codes, combat tactics, communications ciphers. The ships that resisted were destroyed. The rest surrendered.

The Yeerk crews were shuttled to the Pool ship where they left their host bodies to return to the now-refilled pool. Newly freed human and Hork-Bajir worked with Andalites to keep the ships flying.

Jake had one more run-in with Asculan over possession of the great trophy prisoner, Visser One. But Jake won that confrontation, too. Visser One remained our prisoner.

We Animorphs and the newly minted Prince Aximili, with our prisoner, landed Ax's official liaison ship, a sleek Fast-Courier, right in the middle of the Mall in Washington. Not a mall, *the* Mall, a sort of open green space with the Capitol Building at one end, the Smithsonian Institution and various government buildings on both sides, and the obelisk of the Washington Monument at the far end.

We called ahead, not wanting to terrify anyone. There were roughly a thousand cops and twice that many newspeople waiting for us.

It was, as Marco said, a "shiver-my-spine moment."

A sea of microphones and video cameras and flashbulbs. Ax and Jake, and to a lesser extent Marco and I, gave a sort of brief explanation of what had been happening, and where things stood now.

Needless to say, it was kind of a big news day.

Tobias was silent throughout. If he even heard the questions he didn't show it. And then, as Marco was telling yet another amusing anecdote, Tobias spread his wings, caught an updraft, and flew away.

The next day an Andalite scout ship reported finding a human body floating in space. Young, female. The Blade ship had jettisoned her body before going into Zero space.

The Andalites brought her to California. Near the devastation that was all that was left of our homes.

I was there when Rachel returned. Her mother was there, too. The Andalites treated her body with great respect. She had been wrapped in some sort of soft cloth. I guess it was the Andalite way.

They uncovered her face and Rachel's mom and I identified her.

Two days later, Rachel's body was cremated. It was inconceivable that she'd ever want to be buried in the ground. She ended up as a few handfuls of ashes in a pretty china urn.

Everyone was at the memorial ceremony. By this point our story had swept the planet. Everyone alive knew our names.

The memorial had to be held outside. Fortunately it was a nice day. You could see the Pacific

Ocean from the spot in the cemetery where Rachel's monument would be placed. There was an honor guard of free Hork-Bajir. Two dozen Andalite warriors stood at attention. Our friend and ally General Doubleday was there and quite a few men and women in uniform.

Jake and Marco and me and Ax. We all gave little speeches. The President of the United States was there. He gave a speech, too.

I guess Rachel would have liked it, in her own way. She would have laughed. She would have thought it was all way over the top, but at the same time, she would have liked the attention.

Would have, but she was a few ounces of ash in a jar resting inside an open wooden box.

The ceremony was almost over when I saw him. I'd been watching the sky. I knew if he was still alive, he would come.

He wheeled high overhead, riding a thermal. His hawk eyes would see everything of course, even from half a mile up.

But as the band played some horribly depressing music, down he came. He swooped down and landed on the box, wings flaring. One of the ushers moved to chase him off. Jake took the man's arm.

Tobias closed his talons around the urn's small handle. He glared fiercely at Rachel's mom. She was crying, had been all along. She sobbed and nodded her head, giving her permission.

Then Tobias looked at me. I said, "Yes, Tobias. She would want it."

I don't know where he found the strength to lift that urn, but he did. He flew away, low at first, then, catching a thermal, he bore the urn away into the sky.

CHAPTER 10

Marco

ONE YEAR LATER

My career was going pretty well. I was past the point of being a fad, anyway. I'd done seven appearances total on Letterman and Leno, plus several times each on Jon Stewart and Conan. The *Today Show*, *Good Morning America*, *Oprah*? Been there. Bill O'Reilly called me a genuine American hero. I'd been on CNN so many times that Greta Van Susteren and I were practically roommates. Guest-VJ on MTV? Of course.

And all of that is over and above the rounds of interviews that came in that first wild month after the defeat of the Yeerks. I mean, in that first month you couldn't keep track of how many shows I'd been on. Jake and Cassie and I were bigger than all of Hollywood, D.C., and Manhat-

63

tan put together. We weren't just celebrities, we were the only celebrities. We had senators and big-league rap producers and hot starlets fetching us sodas and Kit Kat bars.

So cool.

That first month we owned the world. But that was the easy part: We had a story to tell and everyone wanted the details of how we and our weird alien friend and all our animal morphs had saved the world. The tough part was to keep it going after we stopped being The New Thing.

I had become the unofficial spokesman for the Animorphs. Jake wasn't interested in doing it. Neither was Cassie. And as for Tobias, well, no one had seen him or heard from him since Rachel's funeral.

It wasn't that Jake and Cassie never gave interviews, but Jake was too serious and heavy for the media. Jake was on his way to becoming this icon, this national hero figure. He had that whole tragic-hero thing going on. People knew about him sending his cousin to take out his brother and they ate it up. I am not kidding when I say that some congressperson actually suggested carving his face onto Mount Rushmore. Nothing came of that, fortunately.

So, anyway, everyone acted like they wanted Jake to do their show, but Jake wasn't really into that game and the bookers for the shows knew it. Jake did not do good panel. He wouldn't sit there and trade jokes with Dave. There was too much he didn't want to talk about. Jake was still carrying the world on his shoulders, and it showed.

As for Cassie, well, she was worse, if that's possible. She had the tendency to wander around in all the moral subtext of everything. She'd take some story about a cool, rock 'em sock 'em battle we'd been in and turn it into this mope about the morality of self-defense.

So basically, with neither of those two being, shall we say, *Hollywood,* that job fell to me.

Bread and butter, baby. Could I do panel? Sure I could do panel. I was as much of a hero as any of the Animorphs and unlike Jake the Yeerk-Killer and Saint Cassie, I was fun.

I got a gig as "technical advisor" to a Spielberg movie about us. *Animorph.* Come on, you gotta love that. I did all the shows to plug that deal. Sample dialog: "I loved working with Steven, he is absolutely devoted to accuracy, and I knew he was the man who could be trusted with our story."

I wrote a book, with some help from a ghostwriter. The title was *The Gorilla Speaks.* Number one on *The New York Times* best-seller list, number one on the *PW* list, number one on the Web.

Cassie wrote a book, too: *Insights on the Animal Mind*. I think it topped out around number seven. Not that I'm competitive.

I had just been signed for a regular acting job. I was going to be Nick Lang, a wisecracking mutant superhero sort of guy who can turn into animals. I wasn't the main star, I was the main supporting player, (and the main special effect), which is what I wanted: I needed time to "work on my craft" without the pressure of carrying the entire TV show. We were going to be on Fox in the old *X-Files* time slot, which was kind of cool.

The acting job was especially great because it kept me alive as a product spokesman. I had a three-year deal with Pepsi, plus smaller deals with Alamo Rent A Car and Gap/Old Navy. You would not believe the money.

So, a year after the end, I was seventeen and rich from book deals and product endorsements and acting contracts. I had a beach house in Santa Barbara (close to Hollywood, but with less traffic) and an apartment in New York. I owned a canary-yellow Viper, a red Maserati, and a desert-camouflage Humvee. I dated girls who wouldn't have looked at me before. I ate in cool restaurants.

And maybe you're expecting me to say it was all an empty experience, that my life wasn't all that great, but you know what? I was happy.

We all should have been happy. Cassie was

Undersecretary of the Interior for Resident Aliens. It paid less than I spend on corn chips, but hey, Cassie was seventeen, like me, and she was meeting with the President and spending most of her time with the free Hork-Bajir. They'd been given Yellowstone as a habitat. They lived on bark and cared for the trees and the tourists loved it. Yellowstone was so mobbed with tourists wanting to see Hork-Bajir swinging from the redwoods or whatever that there was a year-and-a-half waiting list to get in.

Arbron's Taxxons — those that had survived the battle — had fulfilled another of Cassie's far-seeing dreams: They had, as agreed, permanently morphed to anaconda and various other way-too-big snakes. They'd been relocated to the Brazilian rain forest, which was now protected by Brazilian law and hefty U.N. payments. If you were a guinea pig walking around the rain forest now you were toast, but the former Taxxons left people alone.

Arbron himself went down there with them. He could not morph again, of course. He was an Andalite *nothlit*. Many years ago, far away, he had stayed too long in Taxxon morph and had been unable to demorph. And now he was Taxxon for good.

Arbron was shot and killed by poachers. It was a big incident for a while. They caught the poachers and put them away. Everyone said how terrible it was. But you know, Arbron was probably grateful. He had saved his adopted people, but he had been a prisoner of that awful Taxxon hunger, and that's no way to live.

The Andalite ambassador to the United Nations took charge of the body — what was left of it. Arbron was flown back to the Andalite home world and given a quiet funeral.

Anyway, Cassie was a government pooh-bah, always racing around here and there in government jets and helicopters, making sure Toby and her people were good and just generally saving the world. Also taking college courses at night because she still wants to be a veterinarian like her mom and dad. That's Cassie for you: Save the rain forest, save some cow with a hernia — the girl just does not get the whole celebrity thing. I mean Wal-Mart practically begged her on hands and knees to take a million dollars to do ads for their jeans, and she said she didn't have time because there was some controversy over an access road into some forest somewhere.

It boggles my mind.

And Ax was doing great as well. He was an official prince and this huge hero back on his home planet. He had stepped out of Elfangor's shadow at long last, and was not only a hero but the one and only expert on all things human.

Andalite tourism was the coming thing. The numbers were limited — interstellar travel isn't cheap, you know. But the big thing was for wealthy or influential Andalites to come to Earth and acquire human morphs. Then it was off to the mall food courts to raid the Cinnabon and Mrs. Fields.

I am not kidding. An Andalite with a mouth is a dangerous thing when there are cinnamon buns around. Having no mouths or sense of smell themselves, they have no natural defenses against the appeal of flavor — as we had witnessed time and again with the Ax-man himself. You do not want to get between a newly morphed Andalite tourist and a chocolate chip cookie.

Andalites and humans mostly got along well. Andalite civilians are about three degrees more humble and lovable than the Andalite warriors we'd always met.

Some people had been afraid the news that aliens were real would freak the entire human race. They were wrong. Duh. Humans had been watching *Star Trek* and *Star Wars* and reading Heinlein and Simmons and Orson Scott Card for too many years. Humans weren't freaked by aliens — they'd been expecting them for years and were just relieved they weren't The Borg.

Ax worked out technology-transfer deals with some of the big corporations. They have to keep it slow because if you just dump a hundred years of technological advances overnight the stock market goes nuts. It worked out okay, though. The Andalites can definitely teach us a lot about computer architecture. But it was Microsoft and Sony and Adobe and Nintendo that came up with the killer apps. I mean, the new Palm Pilots will be actual pilots.

The Andalites flatly refused to let us share their weapons technology. But NASA has had a definite revival: The first human Zero-space vehicle will be built jointly by Boeing and Lockheed and be ready for launch in three years. H. sapiens was going to the stars. Look out, universe, we're coming to build a Starbucks near you.

As for Jake, well, my boy Jake has always had a serious side to him. I mean, I tried to talk to him about things. But some guys shake off a war and move on, and other guys don't.

Jake carried Tom and Rachel and those seventeen thousand Yeerks around his neck like the Ancient Mariner and his albatross.

Being Jake he didn't lose it. He didn't go off and become some kind of drug addict or have some big breakdown or whatever. He was still Jake. But he was a different Jake. Smaller and bigger at the same time, if that makes any sense. He was closed off, inward. He would sound almost like the old Jake sometimes but you just got this sense that he was out of phase with everyone else. Like he was a half step ahead or behind.

Of course this just made him into the strong and silent type and he always was a big, good-looking guy, so he got marriage proposals (and other proposals) from girls as young as twelve and women old enough to be his grandmother.

No interest.

He loved Cassie, of course, but I don't know what happened there. I know when I talk to Cassie I ask her if she's seen him and the answer is always no. The same when I talk to Jake, although he always says he's just about to call her, just about to.

Write a book? No thanks.

Endorsements? No thanks.

Every college on the planet tried to recruit him. No thanks. West Point offered him a gig as an instructor in the Tactical Application of Emerging Technologies and Xeno-Warfare. No thanks. If he'd been old enough he could have run for president as the candidate of Democrats and Republicans both. Jake was the biggest hero the world had ever seen because he was a hero for all humans, not one nation. He had saved the lives and freedom of the entire human race. I mean, he could have snapped his fingers and had anything he wanted.

The problem was, he didn't want anything.

Except for Tobias to come back. For Rachel and Tom to be alive. For the chance to unlive one fateful moment when he gave the order that doomed seventeen thousand defenseless Yeerks.

I worried about him.

Okay, I worried about him while sitting by my pool or driving my Maserati or escorting some bubbly Hollywood honey past the rope line at the most exclusive clubs. I worried about him.

I hadn't seen Jake or Cassie in a couple of months when my lawyer called to say the date had been set.

And now, the three of us would be together again. In The Hague, Netherlands.

We were to testify in the war crimes trial of the Yeerk prisoner, Visser One.

CHAPTER 11

Cassie

"Is Jake here yet?" I asked Marco. I figured I might as well find out right away. I wasn't eager to see Jake. I mean, yes, I was. But the Jake I was eager to see might not even exist anymore. The Jake I wanted to see was the one who had talked about us being together after the war was over.

The war was over. We weren't together. Now, this reunion was just bound to be awkward if not painful.

"I haven't seen him," Marco said.

"When did you get here?"

"Here?" Marco looked around, puzzled. We were in the modern lobby of one of The Hague's best hotels. "Oh, here at the hotel? I'm not stay-

73

ing at the hotel. My business manager set me up in a rented villa. There's a fence, a gate, it's easier to keep the groupies away."

I laughed and he grinned in response. "You're actually completely serious, aren't you?" I asked.

"Cassie, how long have you known me? Am I ever *completely* serious?"

I felt a wave of affection for Marco. We had never been the closest of the Animorphs — our connection went through Jake, it wasn't direct. But here we were, in some way the only two real survivors. We had even prospered. Each of us was far better off by most measures than we'd have been without the war.

"Is Jake staying at this hotel?" I asked.

Marco nodded. Then, with sudden fire, he said, "I wish he would see you, Cassie. You're what he needs. I mean, I try and talk to him but you know Jake, he can go totally opaque when he wants to. You ask him if he's okay, he says, 'Sure.' You ask him if he needs anything, it's 'No, I'm good.' But he never seems to do anything. Not that I know of anyway."

"How often do you see him?" I asked.

Marco started to answer, stopped, gave a guilty shrug. "Officially? As in, I see him and he sees me?"

"Ah. You're spying on him?"

"I'm still an Animorph. I still like to fly.

Maybe I'm in eagle morph and I happen to see him."

"So how is he, really?"

"I'm not exactly a psychiatrist, Cassie."

I wasn't going to accept that. "Marco, you have a very subtle mind and you're a good observer. And he's your best friend."

The waitress brought us beverages and a plate of some kind of snack. She gave us the familiar "I know you!" smile and left only reluctantly.

"She wants me," Marco said. Then, realizing that I wasn't going to be diverted, he sighed and said, "Like I say, I'm no psychiatrist. But he's depressed. You know, like not just sad but something deeper? Like clinically depressed. Like a party balloon with half the helium gone. Like a flashlight with low batteries. He hangs around the house with his mom and dad. Sometimes he'll go for a drive — you know, at least he kept the free Jaguar. I mean, if he'd refused that I'd have had to kill him personally. And," Marco added with a significant look, "he goes to see *her*."

I knew who Marco meant by "her."

"He doesn't put flowers on the memorial or whatever, there are always lots of those. He goes when no one's around, late, after hours. The guys at the gate let him in. He parks and just kind of sits there like he's hanging out with her. I don't think he talks to her. Sad as it is to say, I wish he did. Talking to a dead person is better than not talking at all. He sits there for an hour, sometimes two, stares out at the ocean. Watches the sun go down. Then he leaves. Sometimes I think he's waiting there hoping Tobias will show up."

Tears were welling in my eyes. The image was too sad. I'd been to Rachel's memorial too. But not like that. "Rachel would be so mad at him."

"Yeah," Marco agreed. "Get over it. Shake it off. That's what she'd say."

"You think that's what he should do? Shake it off?"

"Don't you?"

I wasn't sure what I thought. "Sometimes I'm ashamed that I have moved on, you know? I guess I wonder if there's something wrong with me when I enjoy the day, or enjoy my job or my classes."

"You still morph?" Marco asked.

The question surprised me. "Yeah. Of course. I . . . I don't know, I guess I couldn't see why I shouldn't. It helps with my job. It's just easier getting around way back in the woods if I'm flying, or in wolf morph."

"I can't be sure, but I have this feeling Jake hasn't morphed since . . . since."

"It gives you a different perspective," I said. "I mean, I've often wondered if allowing someone to morph to dolphin or falcon or whatever might not be a good way to let them put the little stuff in perspective."

"Morph therapy? I think I feel another best-selling book coming on. Oh, man, Oprah would eat that up. And you know the Andalites are saying now they may make morphing technology more widely available on Earth."

I frowned. "Really? Why?"

"They want a Krispy Kreme franchise back on the home world. You have a fair number of Andalites who possess a human morph now, all back home after their tour on Earth. Still looking for a donut."

The idea was so absurd I had to laugh. "We're going to trade donuts for morphing technology?"

Marco and I sat there in silent enjoyment for a moment, sipping our Oranginas.

"I think you're right," Marco said after a while.

"About what?"

"Morph therapy. I think it could be useful when someone is in a funk, let's say."

I looked at him to see whether he was kidding. He looked back. All of a sudden neither of us was kidding.

CHAPTER 12

Jake

" . . . Did conspire to subjugate the people of Earth through subversion, terror, and violence. Four. That the defendant did conspire to overthrow all legitimate forms of government through subversion, terror, and violence. Five. That the defendant did commit numerous acts of attempted murder. Six. That the defendant committed murder in the specifics contained in appendix 2C. Seven. That the defendant committed or caused to be committed numerous acts of torture in the specifics contained in appendix 2D. Eight. That the defendant did . . ."

The reading of Visser One's indictment was going to take a while. The War-Crimes Tribunal didn't have a death penalty, just prison. The prosecutors said he was eligible for something like eight hundred years in prison. And since they had about a hundred witnesses drawn from former human-Controllers, Hork-Bajir, and we Animorphs, there wasn't much question about the outcome.

Alloran would not be allowed to testify. It came too close to being self-incrimination, the courts said.

It had taken a year to organize the trial. The biggest problem was how to have the accused be present and involved in the proceedings. There was no way the visser could be allowed to take a host body. I mean, how does a court order one of the very things it considers a crime?

Fortunately Ax's people were willing to help. Very willing. Andalite technicians created a Yeerk box. It was about the size of a hardcover book. It contained a miniaturized Kandrona source, a computer-interface, and a voice synthesizer. The visser could hear and "see" and speak. The box, painted lavender for some obscure Andalite reason, sat on a pedestal facing the curved judges' bench.

There was a panel of five judges, American, Dutch, Chinese, Kenyan, and Chilean.

The visser had half a dozen appointed lawyers. They looked very professional, very slick, and like they knew they had zero chance.

There was a gallery down one side of the

courtroom for media. They had crammed what looked like a hundred cameras of every conceivable type into a space smaller than a men's room.

The whole world was watching. We were live on every station everywhere.

The building was ringed with security. Probably half the people sitting in the audience were security or intelligence people. American, French, British, Russian, Chinese, Indian, Israeli . . . it was like a security convention. And that wasn't even counting the overt security inside the room, a dozen heavily armed Dutch Special Forces guys.

People were very determined that the visser not escape.

Marco leaned close and whispered, "If anyone so much as farts there's going to be about ten thousand rounds fired off before you can say, 'It wasn't me!'"

I smiled.

Marco was enjoying this. But then, he enjoyed the attention. If he made it through his testimony without making a dozen bad jokes I'd be amazed.

Cassie was sitting just beyond him. We had exchanged smiles and awkward hugs. I had dreaded this for months. I didn't know what to say to her. I didn't seem to know what to say to anyone lately. Maybe I was getting stupid in my old age.

Part of me wanted what we'd had in the old days, Cassie and me. But that wasn't possible. I knew that. I had come to accept that all of that, all of what I'd had with Cassie, Tobias, Ax, even Marco, all of it was "in the war." And the things that were "in the war" didn't seem to translate into real life. Like they were written in incompatible computer languages or something.

I still cared for Cassie, for all of them. I always would. My life was divided into three parts: before, during, and after the war. And that middle section was so overwhelming, so big, so intense, it made the other two portions seem dim and dark and dull.

That's how I felt now, pretty much all the time. Dark. Dull. Slow and stupid. Distracted, but not by anything in particular. Just like there was something else I should be thinking about but I couldn't recall what it was.

I understood Tobias. I didn't think he ran away out of rage or even out of grief. I mean, maybe at first, yeah, but I wondered if maybe, like me, he wasn't just looking for simplicity. Maybe.

Why wasn't Marco like that? He thrived on it all. The attention, the fame, the excitement. Maybe he was just more resilient.

81

Ax was to my right. Not sitting, they had removed chairs so he and Alloran and an official Andalite legal observer named Salawan could stand comfortably.

". . . mayhem. Sixteen. That the defendant did perform medical experiments upon human subjects without permission. Seventeen. That the defendant did drive more than a million people from their homes. Eighteen. That the defendant did . . ."

I wondered what the visser thought of all this. It was a very un-Yeerkish scene. The Yeerks reserved trials only for the highest-ranking officers. And they would certainly never try a member of a different species. They had quicker, more direct ways of dealing with aliens.

Suddenly the reading of the indictment was over. The prosecution was ready to call its first witness.

"We call Jake Berenson."

I stood up. My legs were stiff from sitting.

I walked to the front and sat down in a chair placed in a little booth so that I faced the judges and the defendant. It seemed odd to see Alloran, the face I associated with Visser One, standing behind the prosecution desk, free, while my enemy was represented by a blank lavender box.

"The defense objects to this witness."

A murmur through the courtroom. Visser One's

head lawyer was on her feet looking nervous and smug at the same time.

The president of the court, the Chilean judge, leaned forward. "What is the nature of your objection?"

"Your honor, this witness should himself be under indictment as a war criminal. If the alleged war crimes of the Yeerk military officer, Visser One, are to be tried in this court, it must be in the pursuit of impartial justice. Truly impartial justice cannot be applied only against one side in a conflict. If my client is to be tried for his actions in the human-Yeerk war, then so must the actions of this witness. With all due respect to this court, this witness is a mass murderer. A war criminal."

The objection was denied. My testimony was to proceed. But I found I couldn't speak. I felt like I was choking, like the air wouldn't come.

Billions of people were watching my reaction. Billions of people saw me freeze. Billions of people thought, *This is the famous Jake the Yeerk-Killer? He doesn't look like much.*

"Apparently the witness is having some difficulty," Visser One's lawyer said with only the slightest smirk.

"The witness is disconcerted by this unjustified and vicious assault," the prosecutor said heatedly.

The Chinese judge asked if I needed a moment to compose myself.

"No," I said. "I'm ready." But I wasn't. I was fighting the urge to run from the room.

"State your name and occupation, for the record."

"Um, Jake Berenson. My occupation? I guess I'm unemployed."

"Are you a student?" the prosecutor suggested helpfully.

"No. Not really."

"All right. Please tell the court how you first became aware of the presence on Earth of the Yeerk species."

"All right," I said. But then memory crowded in and pushed the court into the shadows. I remembered being at the mall with Marco and Tobias. We ran into Rachel and Cassie. We decided to walk home together. We decided to take a shortcut through the construction site.

A light in the sky.

The Andalite fighter. The wounded alien creature, the Andalite, staggering, falling.

The attack of the Yeerks. Chapman.

Seeing Tobias morph to a cat.

My first morph.

My first battle. The Yeerk pool.

The realization that Tom was one of them.

The decision, not my decision, that I was the

leader. Marco inventing the name: Animorphs. Leader of the Animorphs.

The tiger. My battle morph so many times. So many battles.

The prosecutor prodded me with questions. I answered them. But memories filled the courtroom. I couldn't get them out of my head. And each question triggered more.

When they adjourned for the day I didn't notice at first. I'd been on the stand for just an hour, I had barely begun my testimony. And then would come cross-examination.

What was the matter with me? I knew I was screwed up. I knew I'd made a fool of myself. I'd let everyone down.

I left the courtroom straightaway and found my way back to my hotel room. I sat on the bed and just held my head in my hands and stared. I don't know how long.

I heard a noise. I looked up.

A gorilla.

Marco, of course. Cassie was demorphing, rising from the carpet in one corner. Out of the corner of my eye I saw Ax.

<Hey, Jake,> Marco said.

Then he swung his cinder block gorilla fist into the side of my head.

CHAPTER 13

Jake

I woke up falling.

"Aaaahhhh!"

Not a long fall, but it was into water, into waves, into dark gray waves topped with foam.

I hit facedown and sank maybe ten feet down.

Salt water in my mouth, down my throat. It was freezing. Brutal cold, shocking cold. I wasn't groggy anymore, I was wide-awake, but disoriented. Which way was up?

Sunlight. Cold and far, far away. I kicked madly, moved with painful slowness. Could I even reach the surface? I was a slug. My clothing billowed and knotted around me, twisted me, hampered my movements. Shoes full of water, like lead weights.

I kicked hard and started to rise. I ripped off my shirt, buttons twirling away in the water. I took my shoes off. I was going to freeze to death.

Then, air!

I sucked in deep, spit water, breathed again. A wave crashed over me, buried me, turned me upside down. Then, air again. But air wasn't enough. I was freezing. I couldn't see anything down in the valley between waves. No boat, no shore, no plane. How had I ended up here?

Already couldn't feel my fingers. Thought slowing.

Dolphin. That was it, dolphin. I reached for the DNA that still flowed through my veins.

I felt the changes begin. My skin was as gray as a corpse's. My hair was gone. My numb fingers were melting together, webbing, then stretching out to form fins.

My legs twined together like two strands of overcooked spaghetti. The flesh melted, painlessly. I heard the interior sounds of bones shifting, the gloopy sound of organs disappearing or being replaced, relocated.

My mouth and nose pushed out and out, ridiculously far. All at once a hole grew in the back of my neck.

I was no longer cold. I was definitely mad.

I kicked my tail hard, trying to lift my dolphin

87

body high enough to see over the wave tops. Not enough. I would have to jump.

I sucked air through my blowhole and dove down deep. Ten feet, twenty feet, thirty. Down into darkness. I fired a series of clicks and the ultrasonic waves bounced back in patterns that revealed a school of fish behind me at about my same depth. And a hint of something larger at a greater distance.

At thirty feet or so I twisted and began powering toward the surface.

Up like a rocket. Speed was so easy. So easy to kick my tail and fly straight up through the water.

Faster and faster and the bright barrier between sea and sky was right there, shimmering above me, and I blew through it!

I burst from the water and sailed high and for a perfect moment I held sea and sky within me, all encompassed within my brain.

I flew, and I completely forgot to look around.

I splashed down and reminded myself sternly that I had a job. I had to see where I was, figure it out, try and make sense of it all.

Down and down, and up, up, up, into the sky!

<Aaaahhh!>

Again!

Down and up, so fast, as fast as I could go. As high as I could fly.

Again. Again. Again.

The dolphin body was beginning to tire, but I didn't care. I wanted to be tired. I wanted to drain every last ounce of energy from the creature as I flew and splashed and flew again.

Ultrasound now painted the picture of three other dolphins. They were clearly "visible," but they kept their distance.

I swam hard till the dolphin body was worn out. Not easy to wear out a dolphin in the water.

I was not far from the beach. I could see the buildings of The Hague, not at all far off. I headed for shore and beached. I demorphed in the freezing surf and staggered heavy-footed up the beach.

My friends were right behind me. I waited for them. We were wearing our morphing outfits. Like the old days. No shoes, of course, we never had learned how to morph shoes.

There weren't many people on the beach. Just an old couple taking a walk and a woman with her dog.

"I guess you guys think you're clever," I said, squeegeeing water out of my hair.

"More like desperate," Marco said. "You've had your head up your butt for a long time, Jake. Which is your business. Unless it's our business. Like when you screw up testifying against Visser One."

89

I nodded. I couldn't argue. But if they thought the result was me all happy they were wrong.

"She called me a war criminal," I said.

"She's wrong," Cassie said.

"Did what you had to do, man," Marco said. "We all did."

<Jake, it was I who pointed out the possibilities to you,> Ax said. <I pointed out that the Yeerk pool aboard the ship could be drained.>

"Yeah, but I made the call. I pulled the plug. So why don't you tell me: How is that prosecutor wrong? How is Visser One evil and I'm not? I'd really like to know that." I had intended it to be a rhetorical question. I hadn't meant to sound so plaintive.

Cassie took it seriously. "Jake, I've thought a lot about this."

Marco rolled his eyes. "Yeah, we know."

"I've had to think about it because I've done the same things you've done, Jake. You were the leader, but if you're a war criminal then so are we for following you." She shivered. It was cold and the breeze was gusting. "I've had to make my own peace with things I've done."

Despite myself I was hanging on her words. And despite myself I was remembering kissing her.

"Jake, you can't . . ." She took a deep breath. "You can't equate the victim and the perpetrator."

"So as long as you're playing defense it's not possible to commit a war crime?" I asked. "That's pretty close to just saying that the winner makes the rules because it's the winner who writes the history."

She grabbed my arm and searched for my eyes, forcing me to look at her. "No, Jake, it isn't. There are a lot of close calls in history, lots of wars where the blame is evenly split between the sides. This isn't one of them. Before they came to Earth no human ever attacked a Yeerk. No human ever harmed a Yeerk. This one is clear: We are the victims. They made war on us."

"That's good," I said softly. "All of that is good. We have justification. We're the good guys."

Marco said, "That's right, Big Jake, we are."

I nodded. "That's good for the big picture. See, my problem is a little more personal."

<What do you mean?> Ax asked.

"Well, Ax-man, you're right, you did call my attention to the possibilities on the Pool ship. And when you did that I guess I should have thought, *Well, Jake, it's a harsh, terrible thing to do, but you're justified because, after all, you're the victim here.* But that's not what I thought. You know what I thought?"

Cassie released her grip on me. But Marco just took a step up close, right in my face.

"I know what you thought, Jake. You thought *Die, you filthy worms. Feel the fear, Yeerks. Feel the pain. Feel the helplessness.* You wanted them to suffer and the idea of them suffering and dying made you happy. You were thrilled. You were high."

Cassie winced. She looked away.

I said, "Yeah, Marco. That was about it: word for word."

"Well, dude, you don't get to be a war criminal by thinking bad thoughts. It's what was *done*, not what was felt or thought. You have to judge the act. You were acting in self-defense. You were enjoying the fact that you were winning. Two different things."

Cassie seemed less certain. Far less. She seemed ready to join in with Marco, but she couldn't bring herself to do it. She tried to hide it, but there was this look in her eyes, this sideways look at me.

<Prince Jake,> Ax said, giving me back the title he'd given me long ago, <I am not a human. But it seems to me that it is up to your own people to decide the morality of your actions. Their decision seems clear. My people agree with that assessment. We, the Animorphs under your leadership, stopped the Yeerk threat. We saved Earth. We may have saved my people as well, surely we saved many, many Andalite lives.>

I was suddenly exhausted. Worn out all the way, deep down. And everyone had run out of things to say.

After a long, awkward silence I said, "Anyway. That . . ." I gestured out toward the water. I wanted to say that it was the first real joy I had felt since seeing Rachel kill Tom. But there was a wall between me and Cassie. And Marco, well, he's a guy and we guys don't do a lot of emotional stuff with one another. "Anyway. I'll be good tomorrow, on the stand."

CNN: Breaking News.

"We have this just coming in. The five judge panel in The Hague has returned convictions on twenty-two of twenty-five counts of war crimes against the Yeerk, Visser One.

"Visser One, of course, led the Yeerk invasion of Earth and was in command of all Yeerk and allied forces at war's end.

"The decision means that Visser One will almost certainly never be released from the specially constructed prison facility that has been built in Kansas.

"The trial was televised live around the world for three weeks during which time seventy-three witnesses took the stand to substantiate the charges and allegations. Jake Berenson was the first witness, followed by the rest of the living and available Animorphs, and many, many others.

"And now, we're going to go to our CNN legal analyst, Greta Van Susteren, for analysis of this truly unique moment in legal history."

CHAPTER 14

Aximili

TWO YEARS LATER

<Launch two fighters. They are to go in with sensors on full active, no stealth measures. If whoever is hiding behind that moon is peaceful we do not want to sneak up on them. If they are not so peaceful . . . well, let them think they are facing nothing but a pair of careless fighters.>

<Yes, Prince Aximili.>

Even after the last year aboard the *Intrepid,* I sensed that my first officer did not entirely approve of my habit of explaining my actions for the deck crew. It was not usual. Captains typically played the part of far-distant and all-knowing gods. I preferred to continuously train and retrain. The more the deck officers understood, the more they would learn and the more valuable they'd be in a crisis.

95

Not that we'd encountered any crises. Rather we had chased interstellar ghosts and rumors ever since that first, faint intercept that may or may not have been from the Blade ship.

Well, maybe the Blade ship was lurking behind this cold, dark moon at the edge of nowhere, or maybe the Skrit Na freighter had just been confused about what they claimed to have seen.

The Skrit Na did things for their own impenetrable reasons: They had, after all, made a number of trips to Earth, long before the Yeerks had discovered that planet. And what had they done with the people of Earth? Kidnapped them briefly for absurd medical tests, and on occasion killed some Earth creatures called cows. Had any of that had a purpose? Perhaps to the Skrit Na mind, but not to anyone else.

<Fighters away,> my tactical officer reported.

I saw the fighters come into view on the main screen. They lit up their sensors and fired their engines. In seconds they were just bright pinpoints against the moon's dark green backdrop.

<Take us to stage-two alert, just in case,> I ordered. <It never hurts to have everyone know their battle station. And go to silent running.>

<Stage two alert. Silent running,> First Officer Menderash ordered.

Now we were moderately ready in case a "bad

guy" was hiding out there, and we were sensors-down so we didn't glow like a great big radiating beacon.

A window appeared in the main screen. I saw the face of one of the fighter pilots. Fighter pilots have a certain look, easily identifiable, a mix of swagger and competence and pretended boredom. As if playing the role of bait for a Blade ship was just another training run.

<This is fighter one, Calarass reporting.>

<Go ahead,> Menderash responded.

<There's a ship back here, all right, but not the Blade ship. No evidence of the Blade ship or any active, hostile vessel on our sensors.>

I nodded. <What do you have then, Calarass?>

He shrugged. <Unknown, Captain. All I know is that it is very big, it is powered by old-fashioned ion engines, and it has been hit by some kind of energy weapon. Possibly a Dracon beam. I am showing no life signs.>

I stilled the excitement in my hearts. Dracon weapons were widely available throughout the galaxy. The destruction of the Yeerk Empire had spawned a lot of illegal arms trading. And the Blade ship was not the only renegade Yeerk outfit. Still, if it had been a Dracon weapon that at least increased the chances we were on the trail of the Blade ship.

I took a moment to consider. Another lesson for the officers: Unless you're being fired on, think before you act.

<Prepare a boarding party. I will command. F.O.? Full sensor sweep on the unknown vessel. Take us in.>

This sort of mission wasn't supposed to be performed by me. The captain generally stays on the bridge. The T.O. normally led boarding parties. But I was bored. And I knew the T.O. wouldn't argue: I wasn't just the captain or a prince, I was Aximili of Earth. *The* Aximili. A living legend.

I couldn't complain about being bored, of course. The fleet command had given me what was easily the best assignment around. The bulk of the fleet was engaged either in flying blockade around the Yeerk home world, convoying traders back and forth to Earth, or escorting scientific missions.

The *Intrepid* was just about the only ship out "looking for trouble," as Marco might have put it. Every officer in the fleet was jealous of us. Especially now with so many being eased out of service. The fleet's size was being sharply reduced. War's end meant the end of glory and advancement for warriors.

They all had secondary occupations — that was part of our code, that "warrior" was a temporary occupation. You were supposed to want to stop fighting and go home to your meadow and your scoop, back to your peacetime occupation, your family and friends.

I guess some warriors did want all those things. At some level I did, too. But how do you weigh the sharp rush of battle against the slower, more contemplative joys of watching your trees flower?

I left the bridge and went aboard the clumsy-looking boarding craft. It was designed for docking — voluntary or forced — with any conceivable craft. There were four grapples, basically legs of a sort, with the option to use magnetic, adhesive, or intrusive attachment. It was not a fast or well armed or attractive craft. And it had room for only two dozen Andalites, all of us jammed in hoof-to-tail.

The pilot was at pains to handle the craft smoothly, what with me, the Living Legend, being aboard. I was worried he might overcorrect and humiliate himself. He did, and we nicked the side of the bay.

I sighed. As captain I was expected to point out the error. But as the Great Aximili any harsh word from me carried ten times the usual weight.

<Check that stick, Warlatan, the interface may be a bit balky.>

<Yes, Captain.>

I could see the alien vessel now. The two

scout fighters were on-station, one at the bow, one at the stern, armed and ready. Two additional escort fighters kept pace with us, deployed up-and-down.

It was not a type of craft I had ever seen before. It dwarfed even one of the old Dome ships, big as they were. It made my cruiser-class *Intrepid* look like a toy.

It was built in a sort of star-burst pattern. Asymmetrical. As if someone had picked up a few dozen Earth-style habitations they call sky-scrapers and welded the bottoms together. Each skyscraper was different in shape, size, and color, some quite fantastic.

Still, it was easy to see the extrusion that had been blown apart by energy weapons.

My hearts began to beat fast again. How many ships would dare to take on this behemoth? Surely the Blade ship had been here.

F.O. Menderash reported in from the *Intrepid,* which was now in sight of the alien vessel as well. Sensors showed no life signs. However, sensors did show what might be traces of DNA.

I frowned. <DNA? Specifically? Earth origin?>

<The readings are quite possibly inaccurate,> the tactical officer interjected. <The amount of material is very small and the ship, as you can see, Captain, is enormous.>

<Yes, I had noticed that,> I said dryly. <I

want a sensor grid established. Link with all four fighters and the docker with main sensors. Let us see if we can pinpoint this alleged DNA. It would take a year to search that ship on hoof.>

This took a few minutes during which time we drifted closer and closer to the silent behemoth.

<We have a fix,> the T.O. reported. <Now a ninety percent probability that Earth-type DNA is present in one location.>

No one said anything but there was a sort of silent murmur of excitement. Warriors shifted their stance, surreptitiously glanced at the charge indicators on their Shredders, nudged each other.

<Sensors continue to show no life signs,> the First Officer said. <However, Captain, since this is a very unusual situation, perhaps you may wish to reconsider whether the T.O. should be given command of the boarding party. Or myself.>

<You sense danger, First Officer Menderash?>

He hesitated. Then, <Yes.>

<Despite the sensor readings showing this is a dead ship?>

This time more forcefully. <Yes, Captain.>

<So do I. Just the same, here I am, might as well go forward. Take us in for docking. Let us go see what this DNA is.>

CHAPTER 15

Jake

"Controlling the animal mind and instincts are hardest the first time. The instincts can carry you away, especially in prey animals where the fear reflex is overwhelming. After that first time it becomes easier. Which is why you never go into battle with an untested morph."

"But, Professor, you did."

"Yeah, well, I did lots of stupid things, Sergeant Santorelli. I was a kid when I started. I think your respective governments are kind of hoping that you professionals will learn the good habits from me, not the bad ones."

I was instructing a class. My third in the last year. It was a special class of two dozen men and women, chosen from among elite antiterror forces of democratic nations around the world. I had Americans, British, French, Japanese, German, and Norwegian soldiers in this particular class.

Terrorism had grown as a problem. Many of the worst were religious cults convinced that the presence of alien species on Earth was delaying a hoped-for Armageddon. Some were antigovernment paranoids who had convinced themselves that the Andalites were taking over Earth. Others were sort of latter-day racists who simply needed someone to hate and focused on the Hork-Bajir. Then there were the ecology extremists who just hated anything new and technological.

Terrorists had begun to attack Andalite tourists and free Hork-Bajir. And the Andalites had agreed to make a single morphing cube available, on condition that it remain in Andalite custody and be used only for antiterror forces.

We'd always known it was a bad idea to get between an Andalite tourist in human morph and a chocolate chip cookie, a cinnamon bun, or (to the great relief of the beleaguered tobacco industry), old cigarette butts.

On a more serious level, Andalite–Earth trade and tourism were becoming big business. The Andalites liked the status quo as much as humans did.

I needed a job. I needed to do something useful. And I was the reigning expert on using animal morphs for infiltration, surveillance, and combat.

They called me Professor. A joke, obviously, I still hadn't formally graduated from high school. But they had to call me something, these amazingly fit, smart, disciplined men and women, some of whom were twice my age.

Classes were terribly Top Secret, naturally. The "school" was a squat cinder block building in a forgotten corner of the Twenty-nine Palms Marine Corps base. Way out in the California desert. Nothing around.

I lived in Santa Barbara, now. After the trial of Visser One, and endless nagging from Marco (and his agent and manager and assorted Hollywood friends), I finally wrote a book. It was an autobiography, of course. I hated doing it. But it was a way for me to tell people more about Rachel and Tobias, the Forgotten Animorphs, as people called them.

The book made way more money than I needed. I bought a house for my folks and finally moved out on my own. Tom was gone. My hanging around my parents' house till I was thirty wasn't going to bring him back.

Marco lived half a mile from me, in a house about seven times bigger than mine. We'd started hanging out again. And after a while he'd given up arranging dates for me with whatever starlet happened to be willing.

The Defense Department was my official employer and they flew me in a private military jet from Santa Barbara to Twenty-nine every day of class. Flew me back in the evening. I would sit there pretending to work on lesson plans, stare out the window at the sun setting over the Pacific, and watch the birds below.

I had seen red-tailed hawks at times. But there was no way to know.

I spoke to Cassie every couple of months. She was seeing some guy . . . actually, a good guy. I had met him at one of Marco's parties. I couldn't exactly remember his name. He worked for the governor of California on environmental concerns. He and Cassie spent a lot of time working together with the Hork-Bajir in Yellowstone.

It was a Friday, the last day of class for the week and my students were glad to be done with me for a while, and I was glad to be heading home.

My ride was waiting outside the building. They drove me back and forth in a Humvee with all kinds of security — a courtesy befitting my status as an official hero.

I had been given the Presidential Medal of Freedom and a similarly exalted medal from pretty much every nation on Earth. Some before the trial, some more afterward. If I'd suffered anything tangible from having the title of "war criminal" applied to me, I never noticed it. And I'd gotten so I almost didn't notice the security that followed me everywhere since I'd become terrorist target number one.

The Humvee pulled up alongside my parked jet and I waited, as I'd learned to do, for the marine driver to come running around and open my door. The delay gave time for the two security men to jump out and ostentatiously scan the area.

"Kind of hot out today, Professor," the driver said as I climbed out.

"Yeah, but it's a dry heat," I said. "See you Monday, Corporal."

I pushed my sunglasses up on my nose and headed for the plane. Then I stopped. One of the security guys was pressing his earpiece in and listening intently. He raised his wrist and spoke to his walkie-talkie. "Roger that. I'll ask."

"Ask what, Major?" I said.

"Sir, an Andalite has landed, unannounced. He's here on base. Asking for you."

"Prince Aximili?"

"I don't think so, sir. They can bring him straight here if you okay it."

I nodded. "Let's get into the shade, at least."

We waited and after a while a convoy of Humvees appeared through the wavy heat lines of the tarmac. Two Andalites, not one, rode in the horse trailer towed behind a Humvee. These Andalites had never taken offense at this unusual mode of transport, and it worked better than trying to cram them into a car.

The two Andalites descended the ramp. I went to greet them and led them under the plane's wings, out of the sun's direct rays.

<I am Prince Caysath-Winwall-Esgarrouth. This is Menderash-Postill-Fastill. First Officer of the *Intrepid*.>

<Ax's ship? I mean, excuse me, Prince Aximili's ship?>

<Yes,> Caysath confirmed. <Menderash is the only known survivor of the *Intrepid*.>

I guess I looked pretty stupid for a minute as that news sank in.

"Are you telling me Ax is dead?"

Caysath slowly shook his head. It was a habit they learned as part of communicating with humans. <No. He is not *confirmed* dead. Only missing. In fact, we have reason to believe that he may still be alive, but a prisoner.>

"Whose prisoner?" I snapped.

It was Menderash who answered. <The Blade ship.>

CHAPTER 16

Jake

We returned to base so that Menderash could explain. My heart was pounding. My pulse was racing. I was a little embarrassed by my response, but this was Ax, one of us.

One of mine.

Menderash was telling the story.

<We approached the unknown alien vessel. Prince Aximili ordered the docking ship to board at a place near the suspected DNA reading.>

"No life signs?"

<None,> Menderash answered. He was visibly shaken. I realized then that he was carrying the weight of this. I knew the signs. <We ran every sensor reading we know. You have to under-

stand, it is a thousand times easier to detect life signs than to detect a tiny sample of DNA, we were sure the alien vessel was dead-in-space.>

I nodded. "Go ahead."

<The docking was uncomplicated. They grappled and cut through the outer hull. Prince Aximili and a dozen heavily armed warriors boarded. For a while they merely reported back on the interior of the ship. It had clearly been inhabited at some time. But there was no sign of current activity. None. If there had been, I never —>

<Just proceed with the story,> Caysath said gently.

<Of course.> Menderash stopped the agitated quiver of his stalk eyes and forced himself to stand still. <They used handheld sensors to pinpoint the DNA sample. Prince Aximili picked it up, held it. He said, <It is a few hairs. White.> Then, he frowned and said, <No, not truly white. Colorless almost. Hollow.>

I knew what was coming next. I knew the animal with hollow, colorless hairs that from a distance seemed white. Polar bear.

It was a Yeerk with a polar bear morph that had killed Rachel.

<Then the prince shouted for the warriors to draw weapons. He ordered me to raise defenses on the *Intrepid* and go to condition one. A split

second later the alien vessel fired at us. It was a very powerful weapon. They caught us only half ready. See, sensors are less effective when used while defensive force fields are raised. The attack crippled the *Intrepid*. Half our people . . . there were many casualties. Chaos, as you can imagine. Blood. Computers down . . . Communications down . . . The T.O., he was, he was sucked out into space before the force fields could close the breach.>

"The alien vessel, not the Blade ship, fired?" I asked.

<Yes. It was fully operational. Alive. Very much alive. My duty was to the ship. Standing orders were to save the ship. I had no choice but to withdraw. All four fighters were lost. We pulled back. But just before I did, before I could, I heard him. Prince Aximili, the captain. Not by link, but through normal thought-speak. Very weak. Far away.>

"Yes?"

<The doctors believe I suffered a temporary stress reaction. An hallucination. That I was hearing things.>

"What is it you heard, First Officer?"

<Prince Aximili. He said your name. Just your name. *Jake*.>

Both Andalites watched me, waiting to see my reaction. The marine guards in the room with

110

us watched, too. Their envy was obvious. Neither had seen combat.

<And then, the engines went. We lost most life support. We called for help, but . . . Norshk pirates hit us and we couldn't even put up a fight. Help came, but too late. Air gone. Cold.> He lost the thread of his story, looked embarrassed, and fell silent.

Caysath took up the narrative. <Menderash believes the thought-speak cry came from the Blade ship, which emerged from within the alien vessel and fled at top speed. The alien vessel followed the Blade ship and fired repeatedly at the *Intrepid,* which followed for a while. But their engines were damaged and they couldn't keep pace. The Blade ship and the alien vessel then entered *Kelbrid* space.>

"What's that?"

Caysath hesitated. Looked at me with his big, main eyes. Waited.

"Please, wait outside," I told the marines.

Once they were gone, Caysath said, <The *Kelbrid* claim an empire that borders the far reaches of our own territory. They are dangerous. Warlike. Aggressive. But also very trustworthy. We have a treaty with one simple proviso: We do not enter *Kelbrid* space, they do not enter ours.>

"Was this alien vessel a *Kelbrid* ship?"

<We do not know. We have never seen a *Kel-*

111

brid. They, likewise have no direct knowledge of us.>

"Are they in league with the Blade ship?"

<There is no way to know.>

I was getting impatient. "These *Kelbrid* would have reason to want a live Andalite. First rule of intelligence: Know your enemy."

<Yes.>

"So what are you doing about it?"

He looked very closely at me. <Nothing. *We* cannot enter *Kelbrid* space without starting a war. No *Andalite* ship, no *Andalite* warrior could enter *Kelbrid* space. The risk is far too great, even to attempt to rescue Prince Aximili.>

"No *Andalite* ship."

<Absolutely not.>

He was definitely leading me somewhere. Where? Then it hit me. "There must be any number of surrendered Yeerk ships around."

<I believe there are,> he said blandly. <I believe, to name just one example, that there is a Yeerk prototype ship in orbit above us at this very moment. Very fast. Heavily armed. A sort of smaller version of a Blade ship. We think it was a Yeerk attempt to design an *Intrepid*-class ship. Yes, I believe such a ship, a definitely non-Andalite ship, is in orbit at this very moment, fully fueled, fully armed.>

"And who is going to fly it?"

In answer, Menderash began to morph. He was morphing to human.

"He's still an Andalite," I said.

<In two hours, I will no longer be an Andalite,> Menderash said.

CHAPTER 17

Cassie

I was with Ronnie Chambers, my state of California counterpart of sorts. He was the governor's liaison to the Hork-Bajir. We had left our assistants and even my omnipresent security detail behind. We were scouting out a new valley as a possible extension of the Hork-Bajir territory. The Hork-Bajir were a growing population.

It was a hard climb, but we were high above the summer's heat and I had come to really love searching out the endless still-undiscovered secrets of Yellowstone. I was getting to be a hiking jock, even eschewing morphing except in cases of emergency or special need.

I'd spent so much time in hiking boots and wool socks and L.L. Bean plaid shirts that Rachel's entire ongoing satire of my wardrobe would have had to change. Not that I was exactly fashionable, but now, instead of being pestered by Wal-Mart to do endorsements, I was being pestered by Patagonia.

Ronnie was just slightly ahead of me, the slope was very steep and he was digging his feet in very carefully.

I had resisted the whole dating thing for a long time. And I resisted it with Ronnie in particular because we had to work together. Plus he was six years older than me.

But, after The Hague, I knew I had to move on. I wasn't just Cassie the Animorph anymore. I had been moved out of the Interior Department when the new President was elected. She had appointed me instead to the new position of Special Assistant to the President for Resident Aliens. I was nineteen and I was in the President's sub-cabinet.

Of course, yes, I would always be Cassie the Animorph. There was yet another movie coming out about us and my part was going to be played by an actress who was about a foot taller and twenty pounds lighter than me. So there'd be the inevitable "Where are they now?" stories about Jake and Marco and me. And of course the inevitable bogus Tobias sightings.

I really wasn't trying to "Put all that behind

me." I was Cassie the Animorph, always would be. I was in history books, after all. But I had a different life to lead now. I was going forward. At the moment I was going forward uphill toward a pair of very muscular legs.

And then I spotted the falcon.

Don't ask me how I knew. There were occasional peregrines up here, real ones. But I knew.

"Ronnie?" I said.

"Yeah?" He stopped and held on to a sapling. He smiled down at me. "What, you need a break? I told you not to eat those pancakes. I told you they'd slow you down."

I generated a smile that he read as fake.

"What's the matter, Cass?"

"There's a friend of mine coming."

He looked down the hill. Then up. I pointed straight up at the peregrine falcon inscribing circles above us.

"One of *them*?"

"Jake."

"Oh."

Ronnie knew about my relationship with Jake. I'd probably bored him half to death talking about my relationship with Jake. I felt sorry for him — Ronnie was a man's man, smart, confident, decent, funny. But in the public imagination, Jake was still some melding of George

Washington and Patton and Batman. It was impossible not to be a little intimidated by all that.

Ronnie made a thoughtful face and looked around. "You know what? I'll just head toward that outcropping up there. That should be a good observation post. Whenever you're done . . ."

"Thanks, Ronnie."

Jake came spiraling down, then straightened out to land on a fallen log. He hopped off the log and began to demorph as soon as his talons were on the ground.

<Stand in front of me,> he said. <I'm going to roll right down the mountain if I demorph in the wrong order.>

He demorphed without problems. And then, there he was: Jake. Not the old Jake, exactly, a little bigger, an inch or two taller. *Jake as a grown-up,* I thought. But then, no, that was wrong: Jake had been a grown-up for a long time.

"Hi, Cassie."

Jake always called me Cassie. Never Cass like Ronnie did.

"Hi, Jake. Is something the matter?"

He winced, a rueful acknowledgment that only some problem would have brought him to see me.

"It's Ax. Some Andalite bigshot came to see me yesterday. Ax was on a deep-space mission

117

and his ship was attacked. He was taken prisoner."

"Oh, my god," I said, and without thinking grabbed Jake's arm.

"Yeah. It was the Blade ship. It disappeared into some place the Andalites can't follow. Not without triggering a major interstellar war. It's some treaty. No Andalite ships. No Andalites period. Thing is, the Blade ship may have taken Ax across the barrier in order to use his presence there as a trigger, to cause a war between the Andalites and these *Kelbrid*."

I had barely absorbed the information about Ax being in trouble. I was slow on picking up the thread of Jake's statement. Then it dawned.

"They're asking *you* to go after Ax?"

He made a wry smile. "Of course not. That would be a violation of the Andalite-*Kelbrid* treaty. They can't *ask* me to do any such thing. Of course, if I just happened to find a nice, new, gassed-up and ready-to-go captured Yeerk ship, and if I just happened to decide to go off on my own to rescue my friend. . . . well, you get the picture."

"Jake, this sounds . . . I mean, one ship? You're supposed to go into some hostile space with one ship, and rescue Ax from the Blade ship and possibly a whole alien empire?"

"Plus it seems there may be a third, unknown

alien species involved," Jake said. He smiled in a way that was so much like Rachel. That same self-mocking swagger. How had I never noticed that similarity before?

"Marco will be going with me," he added.

"He will? He agreed?"

"No, not yet. I haven't asked him. But he will."

I didn't want to say the words. I didn't want to. But Ax was more than a friend. How many times had he risked his life to save mine? I couldn't count the number of times I'd been down and only his flashing tail had brought me out alive.

"I'll go, too," I said. "I just need a day to wrap things up and . . ."

He was shaking his head. "No, Cassie."

"Look, if it's because of us, because of, you know, you and me, hey, that's separate and apart from saving Ax. Ax is one of us."

"That's not it, Cassie," he said, all the swagger gone now. He was the old, awkward Jake now, struggling to express feelings instead of making lightning decisions. "Look, Cassie, you're doing what you need to do and were born to do. Part of what we won was freedom for the Hork-Bajir people. And a place for them here on Earth. That's something we won. It's in the bank. It's real and it's good and your job is to protect it.

119

Me . . ." He shrugged. "Look, for better or worse, this is what I do. This is what I am, *not* what you are."

"I'm still pretty good in a fight," I said.

He laughed. "Pretty good? Cassie, you're a one-woman army. But you're the soldier who has fought her war and moved on. That's good. It's not me, though. Come on, Cassie, we both know this is a lifeline for me."

I brushed away a tear. I didn't know how I felt. Relieved? Rejected?

"So you just came to say 'good-bye'?" My voice quavered miserably.

"No. I mean, yes, to say good-bye. For now. But also, I came for Tobias."

I stared at him.

"Don't bother to tell me you don't know where he is," Jake said. "I'm sure he's sworn you to secrecy. But you have to ask yourself what's best for Tobias now. Ax was his *shorm*. He has to go, you know that, even if he does hate me."

"He doesn't hate you, Jake. He never did. His heart was broken, that's all. And you know, Tobias never had anyone. No one before Rachel. No mother, really, no father he could ever know. Rachel was the first and only person who ever loved Tobias."

Jake nodded. "Yeah. I know. But Ax was his

friend. So are all of us, even if he doesn't want it that way. So tell me how to find him."

A few minutes later, after watching Jake morph and fly away, I climbed up to where Ronnie waited.

I knew I had said good-bye to Jake forever.

121

CHAPTER 18

Tobias

The world's smartest mouse wiggled his nose at me. Oh, he knew I was watching, all right. He knew.

He was brown, not especially plump or juicy-looking. He had a tail that I had shortened by an inch on a previous encounter. But since that one close call he had outsmarted me every time I'd gone after him.

It was a lesson in humility. I was a red-tailed hawk with the mental powers of a human. I was being out-thought by a mouse. The question was, should I even try? I had a nice perch, all I had to do was spread my wings and swoop right down on him. By all rights he was mine. But he'd been "mine" before, and I'd ended up with talons full of dirt and grass.

I could see him twitching his nose. No, he knew. He was just waiting to mess with me.

<Okay, Old Man Mouse, you live for another day. I'm not falling for it today.>

I shifted my gaze, slowly scanning my meadow. It was a nice meadow. Up-country where the air was clear and clean, and sunny days baked the wildflowers and gave me the updrafts I needed. The bouncing little stream drew plenty of small prey — except for the year before when the drought had just about starved me out. But now the high snowcaps were melting and the stream gurgled along, and the mice and rats and shrews and rabbits and skunks and moles — all the juicy prey animals — were present in abundance. All mine during the daylight hours.

At night the meadow belonged to the owl who lived in the lightning-struck aspen. But he kept his hours and I kept mine, and there was food enough for both of us. The only real competition came from the occasional wolf pack or a lone cougar, but I still had all my morphs available, and it's a rare alpha wolf who'll decide to keep his pack in bear country.

Today, though, I had a different problem: campers. They had set up their tent the night before, across the meadow, right beside the stream. They'd made a safe, careful fire of fallen branches, and they had at least had the decency to dig a slit trench a good distance away from my water supply, so they weren't complete idiots. But I didn't like having them there.

Hikers seldom came to my meadow. It was far from the regular trails and far from the places where they could easily observe Hork-Bajir in the trees. These two were hardcore crunchies, I guess. They followed all the rules and customs, made sure they collected their trash and banked their fire and when the girl played her flute it was with professional skill.

It had bothered me, the flute. It was a favorite instrument for hikers, and was usually played with the skill level you'd expect of a preschooler. But this was different. Last night I'd moved in closer to hear and to see. She had the moves of a professional, the ease, the focus, all that.

The music had reached me and I guess so had she. She didn't look anything like Rachel. And the guy with her didn't look anything like me, obviously. But something about them, the two of them, the couple, they looked like what I thought we'd look like. They were in love, even a hawk could see that. And although a hawk's visual acuity is well-known, fewer people know that we also have extraordinarily good hearing. I could hear the music. I could hear them talk.

I had hoped they'd move on with first light. But they were dawdling, indecisive, as though not sure they wanted to leave my meadow. Well, I could change their minds for them in a hurry if I needed to.

I didn't know what to do. If they stayed another night she would play her flute again. Which shouldn't bother me. But if there's one great lesson to surviving alone, it's this: Don't lie to yourself.

I was all I had, and I had to tell myself the truth, and the truth was that their presence bothered me.

So, as I raised my predatory gaze from Old Man Mouse and saw that the girl was getting ready to drink from the stream, I thought I'd better run them off. I didn't want to feel bad, I wanted to catch myself a nice, plump skunk pup. I didn't want to mope, tortured by miserable, pointless longing.

Then, before I could act, the girl froze. She stared and called softly but urgently to her friend, and pointed.

A Hork-Bajir was leaping from tree to tree. My mood picked up instantly. It was Toby. She had reached her full size now, a big, dangerous-looking goblin.

I opened my wings, skimmed low over Old Man Mouse's burrow, just to keep him on his toes, flapped and skimmed the flower tops toward my Hork-Bajir namesake.

<Hi, Toby. Long time no . . .>

Only then did I see the wolf who trotted along easily beneath the swinging Hork-Bajir. A wolf? Had to be Cassie.

Toby dropped to the ground.

"Hello, Tobias. I hope you are well."

<Tolerable,> I answered guardedly. I landed on a low branch, just above Toby's eye level. The wolf wasn't saying anything yet, but there was no way it was a normal wolf.

"Tobias, I have done something you may disapprove of," Toby said. She was always ridiculously deferential when addressing me. It was a bit silly, what with her being not only the de facto head of the Hork-Bajir, but also, under U.S. law, officially the Governor of the Hork-Bajir Free Colony and a nonvoting observer-member in the House of Representatives.

I could be mad at her or I could trust her. I decided to be both. <All right, who is it?> I demanded sharply.

<It's me, Tobias,> Jake said.

He began to demorph. Now the two campers were snapping pictures like mad and that didn't improve my mood. I yelled at them in thought-speak. <Hey, Ken and Barbie, knock it off. This is my meadow. You want to stay, sit down and stay quiet!>

It was harsh of me, but I had to yell at someone. I was disturbed. Thrown off stride. I hadn't spoken to Jake in years. Not since Rachel . . .

But I was so surprised, so taken aback that I had trouble summoning up the rage I thought I still felt toward him.

He assumed his normal shape. Older than when I'd last seen him. The last of the boy general had disappeared to be replaced by a young man with an old man's eyes.

The campers were barely breathing now, a hundred feet away, staring like nitwits. Of course they'd recognize Jake. And unless they were dumber than I thought, they'd figure out who I was. Even in this very-much-altered world, there weren't a lot of birds who'd yell at you.

<Well, Jake,> I said with what I hoped was a rock-steady thought-speak voice, <what's up with you?>

"I'm doing good," he said.

<You're older.>

"So are you."

<Well, it was fun catching up. Bye.> I spread my wings.

"It's about Ax," Jake said.

I should have flown away. I knew I should

have. But Ax had said I was his *shorm*. It's an Andalite word for someone who is closer than a friend.

During the war we'd both been exiles in the woods, Ax and me. Neither of us had a real home. His family was a billion miles away, mine didn't really exist. Only later did we discover that Ax and I were, because of almost unbelievable circumstances, actually related.

I could fly away. If I didn't, I was trapped. I would be trapped with Jake. Again.

<What about Ax?> I asked.

CHAPTER 19

Marco

I had nine million four hundred and thirty-two thousand dollars in my Merrill Lynch account. Mostly in stocks, some bonds.

My TV show was doing fine, winning its time slot, although viewership in the critical demographic was falling off a little.

I had a girlfriend. She was a model/actress. She was not, shall we say, a genius. But she was beautiful and sweet and about a foot taller than me.

I had seven cars. A butler named Wetherbee. (Actually his name was McPherson, but I liked the sound of 'Wetherbee.') I had two maids. I had a time-share deal on a jet. I had the house in

129

Santa Barbara, the *pied-a-terre* in New York and was looking at a little place in Tuscany.

So exactly why was I spending my time morphing to lobster in order to crawl along the bottom of my swimming pool?

I hadn't done the lobster morph in a long, long time. It seemed like a million years ago I'd used it to escape the Yeerks by hiding in a grocery store's fresh fish tank.

The days, man. Those were the days.

I watched, fascinated, as my skin turned hard. It was cool. Like my fingernails were expanding to cover my entire body. Not red, by the way, no lobster wants to be red because you don't get red until you've been boiled. No, this was more of a mottled blue thing.

My fingers melted together and covered over with blue fingernail and my whole hand began to swell up. Like I'd hit it with a hammer. Then this big mass split in two, separating into the halves of a pincer.

Tiny, waving legs erupted from my diaphragm and that's when the doorbell rang.

Wetherbee would get it and get rid of whatever fan was there for an autograph.

I was just losing my legs and eyes when Jake walked in.

"Well, if it isn't Lobster Boy."

<Hey, Jake. Remember this morph?>

"Uh-huh. Some reason why you're morphing to lobster?"

<Ummmm. . . I dropped my keys down in the pool? I was going to go get them?>

"Well, then it's a good thing you have the ability to turn into a lobster, because otherwise, what would you do? I mean, normal people, they drop their keys in the pool, they're just totally helpless. Those keys stay down there. Forever."

I stopped the morph before I lost my eyes and began to reverse it. As soon as I had a mouth I said, "You seem perky, today. You want something to drink?"

"What are you going to do, morph to cow and squeeze me out a glass of two percent?"

"I take that as a no? Wetherbee? Can you bring out a diet Coke?" I looked closely at Jake. "There's definitely something wrong with you, Jake. You're being way too clever. Way too quick. What's up? You finally go on Prozac?"

He winced a little and I was sorry I'd opened my mouth.

I flopped into a chaise longue and waited. He had something to tell me. Jake has no poker face.

He sat down, too, but on the edge of his seat. He glanced up and smiled a little. I looked up and saw a hawk, circling high in the air, directly above us.

In a heartbeat it was as if everything around me turned translucent, like it was all fake, a set created with the help of trick lighting. Now, with the sudden change, it was like I could see right through the walls of my very nice house. Right past old Wetherbee and the silver tray with my Coke. The last three years were magically reduced to a daydream. An old reality emerged from beneath the illusion.

I reached for my drink and my hand was trembling.

Jake waited, patient now that he knew that I knew. He was watching me, waiting for my reaction. Waiting, but not like he had any doubt about me, the smug jerk.

"You're about to ruin my life, aren't you?" I asked him. I sounded more self-pitying than I'd intended to.

"That depends."

"Yeah, right. So, what is it?"

He told me, and every word was another nail in my coffin because, what was I going to do? Refuse to help save Ax?

At last Tobias swooped down and landed on my patio table.

"So where's the other Horsewoman of the Apocalypse?" I asked.

"Cassie? She's not coming on this one," Jake said.

I nodded. "Good for you. At least you have that much sense."

Jake shrugged. "She's doing what she needs to be doing."

"And I'm not?" I demanded.

He ignored that. Which made me mad, because it's not like what I do for a living is just negligible. Granted what Cassie does is more impressive and admirable, if you care about that, but I had a TV show. I was a millionaire.

"So now you're rounding up the old gang, huh? Like one of those over-the-hill-gunfighters movies? Like our parts should be played by Clint Eastwood and James Garner?" I glanced at Tobias. "And Foghorn Leghorn?"

<Marco, you're not even twenty,> Tobias said. <I'm old, for a red-tail. You, you're not even old enough to drink.>

"Yeah? Well, I aged in gorilla years." I pouted for a moment, very annoyed that neither of them was buying my act at all. And, being annoyed, I lashed out a little.

"You sure you're up for this, Jake? You haven't exactly been living the American Dream since your last war."

That got him, and again I was mad at myself, which made me madder at him.

Jake said, "Well, maybe we live and learn."

"What have you learned?" I challenged. "You've

133

been all depressed, and now you see a way out of it because someone's giving you another chance to play war?"

"Maybe," he admitted softly.

I groaned. Being ticked off was stupid of me. And we had important stuff to discuss.

"Okay, Jake-man. I'll cut the baloney if you will." I leaned toward him. "You're my friend. Ax is my friend. On a good day I can even stand the flea-bitten buzzard here. But you have to get real: You've been messed up behind some hard decisions you made. And now you want to go make more hard decisions?"

Jake glared fiercely. "I learned from my mistakes. This time, maybe I'll do it differently. Some things at least."

Ah, so there it was: Jake was going to give himself another chance. This time he would be the warrior who never sinned. He would be Sir Galahad. I felt sorry for him, and I knew I should probably just shut up. But I was his friend, and a friend tells you the stuff you don't want to hear.

"Okay, Jake, I'm in. I'll go with you. You know that. But here's what you need to realize going in: If you're in charge you're going to end up right back in the same swamp you didn't like the first time."

"Marco, I —"

"Shut up for a minute. Listen. If I'm putting

my life on the line with you again, the price you pay is to listen to me now." I took a deep breath. "Back in the day, Jake, you made more heavy decisions than any ten men would have to in a hundred lifetimes. You made life-and-death calls. You got us up to our butts in alligators, and you got us back out. And, sorry, but it's not what people think, that you were some kind of military genius. I'm better at tactics than you are."

<And humble, too,> Tobias muttered.

"It's true, and Jake knows it," I shot back. "Jake, you won because you didn't scare. You didn't panic, you didn't scare, and you didn't play a part or strike poses wondering what history would think. You made the right calls without regard to all that. But then, when the shooting was all over, you started questioning everything you did. You armchair quarterbacked your entire life and decided you made mistakes. Well, no kidding. Surprise: You're not a god."

Jake nodded. "This time I won't make mistakes."

"Don't tell me that," I said. "You want a zero-screwup fight?"

"I got Rachel killed. Wouldn't you like me to keep that from happening to you?"

"Yeah, I really would. But you start thinking that way, and *that's* when you'll get me killed. You have to trust your instincts, not your doubts.

I'll trust my life to your instincts. If we're fighting again you have to be able to make the same kind of crazy, reckless, ruthless decisions you made before. We beat an empire, my friend, the six of us, and we did it in large part because you didn't know any better than to trust your own instincts."

I stopped talking and Jake didn't say anything. I could tell I'd had no effect on him. Or at least not the effect I'd hoped. All I'd managed to do was send him spiraling back to that awful day aboard the Pool ship.

After a while, he shook himself, smiled and said, "So, you're in, right?"

And of course, I was.

CHAPTER 20

Jake

We drove through the desert night, silent most of the way. Me, Marco, and a human-morphed Tobias crammed in the front seat of a truck borrowed from the Twenty-nine Palms motor pool. A Humvee followed behind us with the now-permanently human Menderash and two volunteers recruited from my counterterrorism class.

I'd put it to the class that I needed volunteers for a mission that would very likely prove suicidal, that was illegal, that would involve their disappearing without a trace, without the approval of their governments, without notice to their families. They wouldn't be paid, promoted, or well-treated. I would be in charge and they would be low men or women on the totem pole.

137

All but three volunteered. It was a measure of my fame, I guess. It made me feel a little bad, like I was taking advantage of them. I decided to take two of them, Sergeant Santorelli, a U.S. Army Ranger who was five years older than me, and a French Deuxième Bureau trainee named Jeanne Gerard. I chose them both on the strength of their lack of any close family.

I could have had more, but I felt six people was the right number. It had worked before.

Unfortunately, Jeanne was beautiful. A problem I should have foreseen.

We hit a hard bump and Marco said, "See? You really should have put Jeanne up here with us. A bump like that might bruise her. I could have protected her."

He made a point of carefully pronouncing her name *Zhann*. I sighed. "This is going to be a problem, isn't it?"

"What? Me and Jeanne? No problem at all. Obviously she wants me, and what woman doesn't? So I don't see any problem at all."

I looked at him. "Marco."

"Yes, Jake."

"If you wanted to chase women you could have stayed home."

"Believe me, I wish I had. I had a good life. I had it all. They're going to have to cancel my show, do you realize that? But, hey, without me

138

who would take care of you and the winged wonder here?"

"Marco, you were bored out of your mind."

"Yes, I was."

"If I hadn't asked you to come you'd have killed me."

"Yes, Jake, I would."

"But that's not going to change the fact that you'll be whining endlessly about the wonderful life you gave up, is it?"

"I really doubt it."

"Uh-huh. What's GPS say?"

Marco peered at the dimly glowing display. "Better turn off your lights. We don't want to just drive up and look like complete amateurs."

I killed the lights and slowed way down. The Humvee followed suit. We drove on till Marco said we were there. I stopped and turned off the engine. In the black desert night I could see a slight glow. It was impossible to tell the distance with no visual points of reference but the GPS said we had only three hundred yards to go.

We climbed out and stretched our legs while the rest of our troop joined us.

I said, "Okay, Santorelli? Jeanne? Call this your first nontraining mission. Our job is very simple but it can be easily screwed up, so pay attention. Ahead is an Andalite shuttle. There are two Andalite crew on board. They've been told to park their craft there and wait for a terrorist turncoat who will bring them vital information. Nothing else. Everything is on strict need-to-know basis."

"Hi, I'm Marco," Marco said to Jeanne. "I have my own TV show."

"Here's the deal: We need to take down these two Andalites but not hurt them in any serious way. Is that crystal clear? A good pop alongside the head and they'll go down. But no cutting, slashing, or stabbing. These are our allies. We want this to look real, but we don't want anyone to go to the hospital."

Everyone understood. Or so they said.

It was all a setup. Caysath had made the arrangements. We needed a ship to reach orbit where we could "steal" the parked Yeerk craft. And the Andalites needed deniability.

After we used the shuttle to reach the Yeerk ship we would crash the shuttle back into the desert. The official story would be that terrorists seized the Andalite shuttle but were unable to fly it and crashed. The two Andalite guards would testify that they were overpowered. The State Department would yell at the Andalite government for being careless. Everyone would be happy.

"Six against two," Jeanne said. "This is perhaps overkill?"

"Keel. Ovair-keel," Marco echoed. "I love your accent."

"They are Andalites," Menderash grated. "Six is hardly enough."

I smiled. "It's all in which morph you choose. Okay, tell you what, we'll do it with just two of us. Tobias? Please demorph and then to Andalite."

It was a test for both of us, Tobias and me. Would he follow my orders? If not, best to find out now. He said nothing. But he began to morph.

A few minutes later the two Andalites on the shuttle thought they heard a thought-speak cry. They opened the hatch to investigate and out in the desert at the limits of their vision, they got the impression of a running Andalite. Maybe it was a wild mustang, but they couldn't be sure so they trained all their eyes forward. It was thanks to this that they didn't see the gorilla drop from the top of the shuttle and knock their heads together.

It was a severely disgruntled Menderash who took the controls of the shuttle as we lifted off. "They were shamefully careless. Andalite warriors taken from behind? Shameful."

"You know, I could be kind of a mentor to you," Marco said to Jeanne. "If we worked closely together I could teach you all I know."

"But what could I possibly do to repay you?" Jeanne asked.

"Well . . ." Marco leered, and was about to offer some specific ideas when Jeanne interrupted him.

"I know! Perhaps someday I could introduce you to my cousin Michelle. She likes short men. Even as short as you."

Marco winced. "Ah. Beautiful and mean. I like you." He caught my eye. "Jake, when you get a minute could you help me pull this knife out of my chest?"

We reached orbit and I watched both Jeanne and Santorelli closely. It was their first time off-planet. Santorelli tried hard to be cool about it but there was no hiding the slow smile of pleasure.

"Cool, huh?" I said, nodding toward the day–night line of Earth far below.

"I've seen it on TV," he said. "This is better."

"Objective locked in, Captain," Menderash reported.

It took me a beat to realize he meant me. "All right. Take us in. Let's see what she looks like."

The ship in orbit was unlike any Yeerk craft I'd seen before. It had the usual air of danger and hostility — the Yeerks favored the tapered, sharp-edged look generally. But in this case the aggressive, muscular silhouette achieved a certain beauty.

It was a quarter the size of a Blade ship, maybe five or six times as big as a standard Bug fighter. The overall impression was of a sharpened boomerang, ends raked forward and ending in nasty-looking Dracon cannon. The core of the ship was a flattened and tapered cylinder placed above this seeming wing.

"It looks tough enough," Marco said.

Menderash said, "It is very fast and packs a very powerful weapons array, for its size. It carries no Bug fighters but does carry two small shuttlecraft. The Yeerks intended these cruiser-class ships to keep track of what they imagined would be a far-flung empire. As well as for escort duty."

"Well, it's ours now," I said. "Okay, Menderash. Let's go aboard."

He hesitated.

"What?" I asked. I had worried from the start that a former Andalite first officer would have a hard time taking orders from me.

"It's nothing, Captain. Just a custom. An Andalite custom. We always name a ship before the first crewman boards — it's an old notion, a superstition, really. The thinking is that the ship must know who *it* is before the crew can know it."

I relaxed. "Fair enough, Menderash. Our own superstition is that a ship is never an 'it,' it's always a 'she.' Even if the ship is named after a male, it's a 'she.'"

The six of us stood there contemplating our

dangerous-looking new home, set against the sunrise over Earth.

"So what do we call her?" Marco wondered.

<She's beautiful,> Tobias said. <She's beautiful and dangerous and exciting.>

I turned in surprise to look at Tobias. He stared back at me with his eternally fierce hawk's gaze.

Marco laughed, realizing what we were thinking. "She would love it. A scary, deadly, cool-looking Yeerk ship on a doomed, suicidal, crazy mission that no one can ever know about? She would love it."

So it was that we went aboard the *Rachel*.

CHAPTER 21

Marco

The *Rachel* was fast.

We blew through normal space and into Zerospace before either of the two Andalite ships in orbit could react.

Later we picked up their Z-space communications. They made a lot of noise about the "theft" of the Yeerk prototype ship. It was almost too much. But I guess they wanted the news to get out: The *Rachel* was not Andalite, not associated with Andalites, not sanctioned by Andalites. Nope. Clean hands and innocent looks all around.

The fact that this Yeerk ship was fully stocked with human food? That the quarters designed for Hork-Bajir had been converted to human proportions? That certain controls designed to be manipulated by Taxxon pincers now perfectly fit human hands? Well, what would the *Kelbrid* ever know about that?

Santorelli and I went to do an inventory of the supplies. We found water, vitamin pills, a good supply of various awful-looking freeze-dried foods and six dozen Cinnabons.

"Do Andalites have a sense of humor?" Santorelli wondered.

"We've never been entirely sure," I said.

The cinnamon buns didn't last long. We spent four days in Zero-space, which is like being buried in marshmallow sauce, and before we reemerged into the familiar universe of black space and white stars, all fresh food was long gone.

Menderash was in charge of piloting and flying the *Rachel*, but Jake wanted as much cross-training as possible, so we all took turns under the *nothlit* Andalite's tutelage. Menderash was a taciturn guy — as I guess you'd expect from an officer who'd lost his entire crew and chosen to permanently abandon his usual body. He was careful to be deferential to Jake, and I think he had real respect for our fearless leader. But when he taught navigation or piloting skills he was a whole different guy. He was like that psycho drill sergeant from *Full Metal Jacket*.

Four days of Menderash and I was a long way from being an Andalite-quality pilot, but I could take the ship from point A to point B. With lots of help from the computer.

Menderash naturally plotted our course. Jake had talked it over with all of us, but it was Menderash who knew the last course taken by the Blade ship, so my opinion was not all that valuable.

The theory was that we would simply draw a straight line. (Well, figuratively straight. Turns out space is curved. Who knew?) And try to jump past the place where the Blade ship would now be, assuming it had continued on its merry way for the last three weeks.

A big assumption, but it was all we had.

We emerged into real space with all guns loaded and the six of us ready for trouble. What we found was a whole lot of nothing. We were six light-years from the nearest planetary system. It was back the way we'd come.

So it was back into Z-space, and throw the ship into reverse. (Menderash grits his teeth when I say things like that.) We popped back out of Z-space practically on top of the second biggest of four planets around a star that was ready to go nova at any minute. And of course, in celestial terms, "any minute" means maybe this millennium, maybe the next.

"This is *Kelbrid* space," Jake said, "so we have to assume that this planet may have *Kelbrid* remote sensors or even a *Kelbrid* outpost. Let's remember that we are a peaceful ship on a mission of exploration."

We spent the next six weeks wandering around the system, seeing some cool things on strange worlds, but no evidence of *Kelbrids*. We were starting to wonder whether there was any such thing as a *Kelbrid*. And we definitely saw no sign of the Blade ship or the mysterious alien craft that had fired on Ax's *Intrepid*. We moved on to the next nearest system. And the next.

Half a year went by, but it seemed longer. I had brought along some DVD's but there are only so many times you can watch *Airplane!*, especially when you have to explain every joke to a former Andalite.

It became obvious that this was going to be a long trip. You can't just go toodling around a billion square light-years and find what you're looking for.

In the end, even after many months, we didn't find the Blade ship. They found us.

I was manning the sensor station (and using the ship's computers to play Tomb Raider V), when I spotted the orange squiggle indicating an unknown ship within range.

"Hey, Menderash, I have a ship here. Um . . . I think they're hailing us. That's the red numbers, right?" It was just the two of us on the bridge, everyone else was either sleeping or eating.

He stalked over and stared at my screen for about a second. Then, "Captain, to the bridge!"

"What is it?" I asked.

But before the Andalite could answer, Jake was there, looking frowzy and flat-haired. He'd been sleeping, I guess.

"What is it?"

"That was *my* question," I muttered.

"Ship approaching in normal space, Captain. They've hailed us. Standard inquiry: our point of origin and destination."

"Okay. Answer them."

We gave out our story, that we were the *Enterprise,* a peaceful, deep-space exploration ship from The United Federation of Planets. We figured no one in this far corner of the universe would have seen *Star Trek* reruns. It was our little joke.

Here was the problem with that thinking: The Yeerks we were chasing had spent years on Earth, many with human hosts.

"Receiving response," Menderash said. "And a request for visual, two-way communication."

<Uh-oh,> Tobias said. He had rushed to the bridge, along with Jeanne and Santorelli.

"What do we show them?" Santorelli wondered.

"Not me," Jake said. "If it's the Blade ship they may recognize me. Or Marco, or Tobias, for that matter." He looked quickly at the faces of his people. "Santorelli, you're the best B.S. artist aside from Marco. So you're the captain. Jeanne, you stand with him. Everyone else out of view. Narrow the audio channel to pick up Santorelli only. Okay, open communications."

The image that appeared to us was of a human. A man, maybe forty years old. Laughing, with hands on hips. "So, you come from the Federation, do you? And where is Captain Picard?"

Santorelli shot a look at Jake. But this was more my specialty than his.

"You've always thought of yourself as more of a Captain Kirk," I whispered.

After that first panicked glance Santorelli betrayed no sign that he was listening to anyone. He assumed a wide, cocky stance and said, "I've always thought of myself as more of a Captain Kirk."

"Sensor confirmation: It's the Blade ship," Menderash hissed.

That tightened a few sphincters.

The Yeerk captain nodded in a genial sort of way in response to Santorelli. "That's quite a ship you have there . . . excuse me, I don't know your name."

I made a slashing gesture with my hand, cutting Santorelli off before he could say something wrong. "You're Rakich-Four-Six-Nine-One of the Flet Niaar Pool."

Santorelli repeated it.

The Yeerks seemed to buy that. "I am Efflit-One-Three-One-Eight of the Sulp Niar Pool," their captain replied. "Well met. And what exactly are you doing here, brother? And how do you come to be flying a new cruiser-class ship?"

"I might ask the same of you," Santorelli shot back. "I find it hard to imagine what business a ship of the Yeerk Empire has in this far-flung quadrant."

Menderash whispered, "He's powering up his weapons and maneuvering to bring them to bear."

"He thinks we're from the Yeerk Empire. Maybe here to hunt him down as a traitor," Jake said quietly.

Efflit 1318, his voice considerably more guarded now, said, "My mission here is classified."

Santorelli nodded skeptically. "As is mine."

For a long moment the two ships were silent. Both had powered weapons. Both were maneuvering for an edge, should firing break out. But in a fight we were toast. We were tough, but we couldn't win against an alert and ready-to-rumble Blade ship. And the real problem was that although we were fast enough to run away, we were aimed toward the Blade ship. We'd have to turn around if we were going to run away, and while we turned, they'd blow big holes in us.

"We have to blink first," Jake said. He gave Santorelli instructions.

Santorelli said, "It occurs to me, Efflit-One-Three-One-Eight, that it would be a tragedy if any misunderstanding occurred here between us."

"Indeed? And what misunderstanding could occur, Rakich-Four-Six-Nine-One?"

Santorelli sighed. He acted the part of a deflated man. "There is no empire, Efflit-One-Three-One-Eight. The empire is finished. I . . . my crew and I seized this ship and escaped as the Andalites closed in. We had heard that a Blade ship had escaped and survived. We have been looking for you ever since. For more than three years."

Efflit nodded. But would he buy it? He and his people were all alone in the universe. We represented the only brother Yeerks he was ever likely to see. Was he lonely enough to be careless? Would he trust us enough to let us destroy him?

"You will place yourself under the command of The One?"

Santorelli's eyebrows shot up. "The who?" he blurted.

I looked at Jake. At Tobias. At Jeanne. There was a sort of collective shrug.

"I command this ship," Efflit 1318 explained, "but I serve at the pleasure of The One Who Is Many. The One Who Is *All*. We are not alone, Rakich-Four-Six-Nine-One. We are not *this* ship alone. We are the seeds of a new empire that will far outshine the old, under the leadership of The One." Weird to see that wild, messianic glow in the eyes of a man you knew was really just a Yeerk slave. It was a disturbingly human expression.

Santorelli said, "Um, who is this . . . this One?"

"I will invoke his presence," the Yeerk said. He closed his eyes and raised his face.

"Okay, this is unexpected," I whispered.

There was a long, silent pause during which time the two ships drew closer and closer. Too close now to do anything but play the game through. If this was a ruse, it was a convincing one. If it was a ruse, we were dead.

I glanced at Jake and wished my heart wasn't jackhammering away.

Suddenly the screen image went blank. The human-Controller was gone.

<What the —> Tobias demanded.

But then the screen glowed to life. More than the screen. The whole front of the bridge was glowing, a light so bright it seemed to shine right through the bulkheads.

Within the searing light, an image appeared. It was alien, not Yeerk. That was to be expected from the Yeerks, they were, after all, parasites, so you never saw the Yeerks themselves.

But there was something very wrong with this particular alien.

The face that filled the screen and more was a shifting image, a slow dissolve from what might be a robot's face, a machine with a rat-trap mouth and steel eyes, into a sweet, feminine, almost elfin visage, and last, and most enduring, into the face of Aximili-Esgarrouth-Isthill.

<Ax?> Tobias whispered.

The face that belonged to our friend Ax split wide open across the bottom and revealed a new-formed mouth full of red-rimmed teeth.

"Save your tricks for this Yeerk fool," The One said. "I see the truth. I see all. Step into view, Jake the Yeerk-Killer. I know you are there, I feel your mind."

There was no doubting that voice. No way to

imagine that it was just bluffing. The sound of it reached deep down inside you, beyond speech, beyond thought-speak.

Jake stepped out in front of Santorelli.

"I'm here," Jake said calmly.

"You have done well to come this far. You have come to find your friend. But the Andalite is part of me now. As you will soon be."

Jake stared back at the foul thing on the screen. I saw what he saw, and I felt as if my brain was shutting down. In that shifting alien face was every corruption, every evil, and such power that it seemed impossible it could be present in just the narrow confines of the onrushing Blade ship.

"Can we shoot?" Jake asked Menderash, making no attempt to conceal his words from the alien.

"His Dracon cannon have longer range and greater power," Menderash reported grimly. "And his defensive fields have been enhanced. I doubt our cannon can penetrate them."

"Thought so," Jake said, still weirdly calm. "But we're faster."

"Yes."

"Okay." Jake took a deep breath. He looked around the bridge at each of us. At Tobias. At me. "What was it, Marco? 'Crazy, reckless, ruthless decisions'?"

I nodded, wishing I had kept my mouth shut.

There was a dangerous smile on Jake's face. Rachel's smile.

"Full emergency power to the engines," Jake said. "Ram the Blade ship."

A LETTER TO THE FANS:

I know, I know, it's rotten of me to leave you hanging at the end like that. But I figured the Animorphs should go out the same way they came in: Fighting.

Well, here it is at long last: the final chapter in the Animorphs story. It began in the summer of 1996. It ends in the summer of 2001. Five years, 54 regular titles, 4 Chronicles, 5 Megamorphs and 2 Alternamorphs. An amazing number of you have read all those books. I am deeply grateful.

I had a lot of fun writing these characters. I know it sounds pretentious to say that I'll miss them, but I will. It seems strange to think that I won't ever again write "My name is . . ." It makes me a little sad to say good-bye to Andalites, Hork-Bajir, Chee, Taxxons, and even Yeerks. It was fun sitting down every day at my computer to invent that strange universe.

There are a bunch of people to thank. (Hey, what is this, an Academy Awards speech?) First of all, Scholastic, in particular Jean Feiwel, Tonya Alicia Martin, and Craig Walker. Also the talented folks who created such great art for the series. And, of course, the people who never get mentioned but who are responsible for the crucial step from publisher to bookstore: the sales and marketing force.

Mostly, I want to thank you guys, the readers. You praised, you complained, you extolled, you demanded, you asked questions that sometimes I couldn't answer. You told your friends, you started Web sites, you sent letters and e-mails, and wrote fan fiction. You pointed out every error I made. You were thoughtful and critical and imaginative. You were loyal.

I want you all to know that it is my choice to end Animorphs. Much as I'll miss it, the time had come. Time to say good-bye, Jake. Good-bye, Cassie. You, too, Tobias and Marco and Ax. Good-bye, Rachel.

And now would be the time for me to say good-bye to you . . . but, I'm off to a new series called Remnants, and I'm hoping I'll see you over there, in that new universe. If not, thanks from the bottom of my heart for everything.

If you're coming along on the next trip, grab onto something because we're going to start off by blowing up the entire world. Then the real trouble will start.

You may now demorph.

— K.A. Applegate

K.A. APPLEGATE
REMNANTS™

1

THE MAYFLOWER PROJECT

Up close, so near Earth, the Rock looked very small. Seventy-six miles in diameter, it was nothing next to the planet measured in thousands of miles.

But, up close, so close, Jobs could see the speed of it. Against the backdrop of space you couldn't sense the awesome speed. But now, as it angled into the atmosphere, in the brief second in which it could be seen outlined against blue ocean, it seemed impossibly fast.

The Rock entered the atmosphere and for a flash became a spectacular special effect: The atmosphere burned, a red gash in its wake.

It struck the western edge of Portugal. Portugal and Spain were hit by a bullet the size of Connecticut. The Iberian peninsula was a trench, a ditch.

The Mediterranean Sea, trillions of gallons of water, exploded into steam. Every living thing in the water, every living thing ashore, was parboiled in an instant.

Portugal, Spain, southern France, all of Italy, the Balkans, the coast of northern Africa, Greece, southern Turkey, all the way to Israel was obliterated in less than five seconds. They were the cradles of Western civilization one second, a hell of super-heated steam and flying rock the next.

The destruction was too swift to believe. In the time Jobs could blink his eyes, Rome and Cairo, Athens and Barcelona, Istanbul and Jerusalem and Damascus were gone. Not reduced to rubble, not crushed, not devastated. This wasn't like war or any disaster humans understood. Rock became gravel, soil melted and fused, water was steam, living flesh was reduced to singed single cells. Nothing recognizable remained.

The impact explosion was a million nuclear bombs going off at once. The rock and soil and waters that had once defined a dozen nations formed a pillar of smoke and flying dirt and steam. The mushroom cloud punched up through the atmosphere, flinging dust and smoke particles clear into space.

Jobs could see a chunk of Earth, some fragment left half intact, maybe twenty miles across, spin slowly up in the maelstrom. There were houses. Buildings. A hint of tilled fields. Rising on the mushroom cloud, flying free, entering space itself.

The entire planet shuddered. It was possible to see it from space: The ground rippled, as if rock and soil were liquid. The shock wave was an earthquake that toppled trees, collapsed every human-built structure around the planet, caused entire mountain chains to crumble.

The oceans rippled in tidal waves a thousand feet high. The Atlantic Ocean rolled into New York and over it, rolled into Charleston and over it, rolled into Miami and washed across the entire state of Florida. The ocean waters lapped against the Appalachian Mountain chains, swamped everything in their way, smothered all who had not been killed by the blast or the shock wave.

People died having no idea why. People were thrown from their beds, dashed against walls that collapsed onto them. People who survived long enough to find themselves buried alive beneath green sea many miles deep.

Jobs saw the planet's rotation slow. The day would stand still for the few who might still be alive.

The impact worked its damage on the fissures and cracks in Earth's crust. Jobs watched the Atlantic Ocean split right down the middle, emptying millions of cubic miles of water as if it was of no more consequence than pulling the plug on a bathroom sink.

The planet was breaking up. Cracking apart. Impossibly deep fissures raced at supersonic speeds around the planet. They cut through the crust, through the mantle, deeper than a thousand Grand Canyons.

Now the Pacific, too, drained away. It emptied into the molten core of Earth Itself. The explosion dwarfed everything that had gone before. As Jobs watched, motionless, crying but not aware of it, Earth broke apart.

It was as if some invisible hand were ripping open an orange. A vast, irregular chunk of Earth separated slowly from the planet, spun sluggishly, slowly away. The sides of this moon-sized wedge scraped against the sides of the gash, gouged up countries, ground down mountains.

And now this wedge of Earth itself broke in half. Jobs saw what might have been California, his home, turn slowly toward the sun. If anyone is left alive, he thought, if anyone is still alive, they'll see the sunrise this one last time.

Earth lay still at last. Perhaps a quarter of the planet was bitten off, drifting away to form a second and a third Earth. The oceans were gone, boiled off into space. The sky was no longer blue but brown, as dirt and dust blotted out the sun. Here and there could still be seen patches of green. But it was impossible to believe, to hope, that any human being had survived.

All of humanity that still lived was aboard the shuttle that now slid slowly toward the distant sun. . . .

Get into
the mind of
K.A. Applegate

Visit
www.scholastic.com/kaapplegate

Learn everything you
need to know about
Animorphs® and *Everworld*™,
and get a sneak peek
at K.A. Applegate's
new series, REMNANTS™,
in bookstores
June 2001.